The Man Lost in Infinity

By Jamshid C. Tavallali

Hello! I am the author of the book and I wanted to give you some helpful tips.

I advise reading the book first and enjoying the story, second time reading the book look for references and Easter eggs which I have hidden, afterwards try solving the locked chapters and find the hidden one.

NOTE: Regarding chapter XLVII, please note that all of the codes are not in the book and you need to search the web and my other projects to find them.

You can find the playlist of the music here:

YouTube: https://www.youtube.com/playlist?list=PLImBqwEePkQ-f5PLx049Jglb5LIjUOZUS

Spotify:
https://open.spotify.com/playlist/6V4RhpjSCLjJoQeGaZMx3q?si=vJybWr4IRyC1tR9uIRFlcg

Or you can purchase the songs from stores.

My next project in the works if you are interested is on: YouTube: @JepicJ

Library of congress cataloging-in-publication Data has been applied for.

TXu002180071 Novel

INDEX

I. Yek

Our story begins in the year 2059 at the Multiverse Dimension Observatory on Planet Earth. A young Caucasian woman between the age of 19 and 21, with long dark brown hair, wearing jeans, a loose shirt, a black hoodie and sneaker, is researching the ongoings of Other Dimensions. She has been noticing for a few days that a few Dimensions have been going "off-grid". This is an aberrant behavior and most unusual. Nevertheless, no one had been listening to her since she did not have enough evidence to support her case. Her closest friends and family call her "Nat"; it is the nickname her father gave her when she was just a little girl.

Now she had enough evidence. She grabbed her coat and tied her hair tightly into a prudish pony-tail and rushed out of her laboratory. She went to the office of the head of Universal Research of United Worlds – the universal-wide research team consisting of the most eminent scientists from around the Universe. It was led by, a Human Being named James. Amongst James's many feats was the curing of all diseases, proving the Multi-verse, opening portals and dimensional portals and many other inventions which he mostly kept to himself....

He was also the first living biological being which went into the Multiverse and explored it with a companion, He came back only a few seconds after leaving but he never said how long he was in there or why he even came back.

Finally, Nat had an appointment with James. As Nat walked up to James's office, a few people came out of his office and Nat entered James' office. James was visibly agitated by the prior meeting. He was wearing a suit and a dapper pochette but no tie, "How may I help you?" he ceremoniously asked.

Nat replied with a smile: "You don't have to be so formal, Dad,"

James laughed and said: "How are you darling?"

"I'm good, fantastic actually. I finally have enough evidence to prove what I am saying," Nat replied.

James sighed and said: "You know that a Dimension can only be destroyed by an external force!"

"I know, I know... but there are more now and there is now an algorithm between them. Look at the pattern. The organization... the manner they're going out by. See it's as if it is a word," Nat replied.

Nat shook the research paper she had in her hand: "See!"

As James was looking at the paper, shiver went down his spine. His face went white, his hands started shaking and he froze in place.

The message was a name. A name that was feared throughout the Multiverse by a select few. The word that had been written was "Key".

Nat seeing her dad was troubled, asked: "What's the matter, Daddy? Why are you so scared? What key is it?"

"It is not an object. It is a name. The name of someone so horrible that calling him a murderer is putting it mildly. It is the name of a monster. The name of someone, who has committed countless genocides of universes just for sport!! It is the name of someone that if you catch its attention he will hurt you or your loved ones in the worst possible way to imagine, both mentally and physically. Every dimension hopper fears that name and when they hear that name they get all defensive because they know they are dead if he gets to you and you'll be in pain every second you are with him and he will not stop until you stop completely," James replied.

James took out a glass put two cubes of ice in it and took out a 100-year-old aged Scotch and poured himself a drink and took a long sip.

"He also goes by different names such as "Glitch", "Dimension Destroyer" but he is infamous by the name of "Key," James continued.

"He killed my friends and I was his target for so long that I was scared to go back home or to make friends or to have any loved ones. Always alone... for so long, until I finally got away from him; a time I wish I could forget," James said.

Nat was saddened by what James said: "You never told me this,"

"I never mentioned it to anyone," James replied.

"I don't want to be a bearer of bad news but the algorithm predicts that after a few more Dimensions our Dimension is next," Nat said.

James looked at the rest of the paper and seeing that she was correct, said: "So he's finally coming for me,"

James, filled with extreme fear, took a noticeably larger sip of his drink and stood up from his seat and walked towards to the window and proceeded to look out into space and said: "And there is nothing we can do about it,"

"Why can't we attack him when he gets here?" Nat asked.

"Because if we do, he'll do something much worse than destroy our universe. He is far too powerful for us. It seems that you don't fathom how dangerous he is," James replied.

Nat hesitantly asked: "So what? Are we just going to wait and die? And not tell the public? They have a right to know!"

James takes another sip from his glass and replied: "Yes that is exactly what we're going to do, and as for the public, they don't need to know about this. It will only cause mass hysteria and chaos. Those that can leave the universe will attempt to do so and it will cause even more attention towards us, and so cause our dimension to be destroyed the sooner than it would be. Those that do escape he will hunt them down destroying those universes to which they fled as well. Because he is so demented that he does not want anything to interfere with his kill streak,"

"But...," Nat replied.

James interrupting her, replied: "No buts, there is nothing we can do!! I truly don't want to do this but we have no choice,"

"There has to be a way! If there's something that you have taught me in my life that is 'everything is possible, no matter how improbable!' So there has to be a way to defeat him. It's the God- damn Multiverse, there's always a way," Nat replied

James chuckled, took another sip and said quietly: "Infinity,"

"What? Can you say that again? I didn't quite catch that," asked Nat. James ran toward his desk and pointed his ring in the middle of the logo on his desk, revealing a hidden computer inside of the desk and proceeded to type and search for something.

"Please say something? What are you doing?" Nat asked.

"There is this one person, one of my friends, he was able to defeat Key but he went dark for years, and now he's completely off the grid. He is the one who saved me. I'm trying to connect to him but I'm having no luck," James replied.

James sighed and laid back on his chair and said: "I would go to the last physical place I know he is at but if I go back to the Multiverse he will instantly know where I am and Key will proceed to destroy this universe. I would send your brother but he's out exploring and as for your other brother, he isn't into Multiverse exploring and, to be honest, he isn't able to go out there in any case. On the other hand, I could send you if you're willing to. You are only 2 years away from the age limit anyway.

"Why me"? Nat said.

"If I sent someone saying they are working for me, my friend will most probably ignore them but if I sent one of my children, like you, there will be a better chance of him accepting you and on the plus side, he could teach you some stuff. He was my teacher too," James replied.

“I know it sounds like really sloppy writing,” James jokingly said

“You think”? Nat replied.

James asked Nat to leave. He had to record a message for his friend in privacy. Nat did so. After recording, James gave Nat a video pen projector containing the video he had recorded.

“So what is his name”? Nat asked.

"Infinity," James replied.

“His parents named him”? Nat asked.

"No, in the Multiverse you do not refer to yourself with your true name, you give yourself a pseudo name or a ‘handle’. Like a ‘nom de guerre’," James replied.

“Why”? Nat asked.

“He will explain,” replied James.

James gave Nat his ring and said: “Do you know what this is?”

"No" Nat replied.

“It’s an advanced dimensional portal opener. It also has some other features but Infinity will explain them later. I have entered the coordination for the last dimension I know he was in. You will know who he is when you arrive there. He is the most powerful person there,” James said.

James hugged and kissed Nat on her forehead and said: “I love you. Go and say bye to your mom. I will explain to her that you are on the way and if you’re unable to stop him don’t come back. Both your mom and I want you to survive. Infinity can protect you,”

Nat was about to leave with tears falling down her face and suddenly ran back and hugged James and said: “I love you too, Daddy!”

James watched her leave longingly and took another sip of his drink. It was already empty. He set it down.

Nat proceeded to do as James said and said good-bye to her mother. She then pointed at a wall and the ring shot out a portal and she went through it and it closed behind her.

II. The King

Nat's portal opens into a kingdom that looked like it was still in the 1500s.

Nat sees a town in the distance with a castle looming above it. Nat proceeds to walk through a valley of strawberries but as she is walking through it she notices that most of the strawberries had already been gathered and packed in wooden crates but were unguarded. This appeared to be quite strange to Nat.

As Nat continued to walk into the town she started to notice a horrible stench. Thereupon, she realized that the portal or her father had set a different time besides the location and dimension. She figured she would be going to the same era but just in a different dimension.

She walks closer and closer to the town. The smell intensifies and gets worse and worse. It smelt like feces. She finally reaches the town. She could see it was a very filthy place. She sees crowds of people begging on the streets, people coughing constantly, dead bodies in stacked piles. It was a horrific sight to behold the state of those people was in such a bad condition, that it made France in 1789 look like a pristine five-star resort.

Since Nat's clothes were somewhat "different" and not quite yet "in-fashion," she was standing out and beginning to catch people's baffled attention.

She walked faster through the town towards the castle. She saw horrific sites -- people in plague masks, as one, looked at her, piles of bodies were burning, women dangled slowly, hung from bridges with "Witch" written on their chests, bruised and bloodied children ran about, with open infected wounds (from a disease they not only knew not how to cure but one which they had not even thought about curing or even questioning what the disease was). Besides seeing, she could also hear snippets that made her appreciate the World she lived in. From the far distance she could hear, "Please Mom wake up," "Pity, pity on the old,""*cough**cough*","*the crackle of fire burning*","*the sound of barn animals*","*the sound of carts moving clumsily around with their load of dead bodies*". The sound though that caught her attention the most and that she eventually saw was the conversation of a few guards with one family. She heard: "I already paid yesterday, I hardly have enough to feed my family, and I truly have nothing to give ya,"

The guard replies, "By the law of the King, you have to give more or it will be taken by force"!

The man replies: "I ain't lying to ya Sir, I truly have nothing"!

"Then we will have your daughter. She will service the Royal guards! Hand her over or she will be taken by force," the guard replied.

The guards attempt to grab his daughter's hands but the man jumps forward stopping them and in doing so one of the guard stabs him with his sword. The anguished cries his daughter, wife and little son could be heard.

Nat's blood boiled. She wanted to do something but she knew that if she did anything it could jeopardize her whole mission. She just closed her eyes firmly and moved on towards the castle.

Nat was fuming. Because she was so angry, it made her stand out even more.

Nat finally arrives at the castle. There is a moat around it, with a giant wooden drawbridge drawn up in the front. The castle looks perfectly carved out of a huge slab of marble stone. The castle is perfectly white. She could see her reflection in the stone. The moat, is filled with water and it was obvious something was lurking in it but she couldn't quite make it out.

Nat, suspecting the King was the person she was supposed to meet, in any case wanted to report the guard's behavior and how they butchered the poor man to him.

Someone from the door yelled: “Who goes there?”

“I’m here to see the King,” Nat replied.

“State your business,” the man replied.

“I am sent here by my father,” Nat replied.

The guard released the drawbridge so that Nat could enter. The door made a great clanking sound followed by big thud as it hit the ground.

Nat walked over across the drawbridge and headed into the castle courtyard. The guard ran towards her and panted: “Welcome Your Highness, the King is awaiting you, and is eager to see you,”

Nat surprised that the King was waiting to see her, rushed towards the Great Hall. The Great Hall had a long red carpet running down its center, with heavy metal chandeliers hanging from the steeply arched ceilings and had perfectly cut mottle stone, with a guard standing every few meters away from one another, in a perfectly organized fashion.

At the head of the Great Hall was a raised stage with a pair of outsized thrones, under a huge and elaborate crystal chandelier. White marble pillars surrounded the back of the throne in a semi-circle, and in the center was a large portrait of the King.

“Please wait as the King shall arrive shortly. He is currently attending to some matters,” said the guard

After 30 minutes of waiting for the King, His Majesty finally arrived, in all his pomp and splendor.

The King was around 45 years of age and had already lost most of his hair.

The King gave Nat a dirty look.

“Ah yes, you must be the Princess of the Far North sent as a token of peace. Very well, I will no longer lay siege to your lands. And to celebrate this bedding let’s have a feast! Guard get her the Tailor and get Her Highness into some proper clothes. I will see you at dinner where we shall dine together," said the King.

And with that, Nat, without even a chance of saying anything was whisked away to a room with her new tailor.

"Ah yes, yes. Come here, Your Highness. Please stand on this stool. His Majesty expects a top-notch dress for you!" exclaimed the tailor.

"I'm okay with my clothes. Thank you very much!!"Nat exclaimed back.

"Nonsense!! A princess like you mustn't wear such rags. It is far too unladylike, replied the tailor".

Nat groaned and said: "I am comfortable in my clothes,"

"Please don't make it hard for me!! They will have my head, if I don't give you a beautiful dress!!" pleaded the tailor.

Nat, somewhat guilt-struck, reluctantly allowed the tailor to make her an elaborate dress. It was a rose pink dress. Not one of Nat's favorite colors.

Nat was escorted to the dining hall. The King was already there, surrounded by his courtiers and a few other women.

"Welcome, welcome. Please make yourself comfortable and enjoy yourself!! We have much planned for tonight, my precious!!" said the King, gleefully rubbing his hands together.

Somewhat taken aback, Nat thought to herself: "There is no way this is to whom Dad has sent me to,"

Servants marched in bearing pile high plates of food, placing it on the tables, in front of each person.

The food consisted of very well-seasoned roast chickens with diced carrots, roasted tomatoes, appropriately lavished with a heavy gravy and had a surprisingly good aroma.

The servants poured red wine into heavy silver goblets. Pastries, cakes, muffins and biscuits were scattered all over the long table.

"So how was your trip, Your Highness? Was everything fair on the way?" asked the King.

"No actually, now that you mention it. While I was coming here I noticed that your guards were harassing some poor man. They killed him and took his daughter, leaving his young son and wife alone. It was very horrific to see!" Nat replied.

"No we can't have that, can we!!I'll tell my guards to be stricter from now on. They should have taken everything he had. And as for the young son, we could always use some more slaves. And as for his wife, she could also have been of service to my men," said the King.

Nat was utterly shocked by the things the King had uttered and cried out: "Do you know about the state your people are in? They are starving! Dying!!"

The King replied in an angry manner: "Bloody useless Sods!! They should be grateful for even living in such a wonderful kingdom!!"

Suddenly a guard came through the doors, rushing to the King and whispered into his ear: "There is someone at the gate, claiming to be the Princess of the Far North,"

The king furiously demanded that Nat be thrown into the dungeon as an imposter. Nat was scared and rose up from her seat. When suddenly....

III. The Strange Man

A guard came for Nat but Nat quickly hurled him on the table, knocking him out in the process. Nat tore her dress so she could move more easily. Another guard lurched and Nat quickly took him down.

"GUARDS!!! Protect your king!" yelled the King.

Suddenly a huge explosion was heard.

"What on earth was that?" yelled the King again.

Screams and shouts could be heard from outside the Hall. From a distance, music could be heard, *bonkers-Dizzy Rascan ft.armand Van Helden*and everyone started to get fuzzy and nauseous. A non-descript man kicked open the doors and the music could be heard even clearer and everything got fuzzier.

A man with a ring, just like that of Nat's father's, with an open white leather-ish trench coat down to his ankles, jeans, and with an untucked shirt stood in the doorway. It could be made out that he was the one singing.

A guard came towards Nat in her now drowsy state but she was still defending herself from another guard. The strange man was going through the guards like they were chips in a bag," Could this man be the person? He is so chaotic" thought Nat to herself.

"How could it possibly be him," Nat wondered.

The man was throwing people all over the walls and taking them down without any thought.

Suddenly the man started dancing as he was and danced up to the king and then put his hand up and the song stopped abruptly and he unexpectedly puked on the King before fainting.

The King, making the most of this now apparent good fortune ordered his remaining guards to take Nat and the strange man to the dungeons below the castle. yelling after them:"I will make you pay dearly!! I will make an example out of both of you".

IV. The Jail

The guards put Nat and the man into one cell and in a grunt tone said: “We will come for you later”

The man instantly went to lie in a corner of the cell, while Nat went to the wooden door with iron bars that was shut on them. The cell was filthy, there was hay on the floor, cobwebs in the corners, a stale wooden bed, a bucket filled with feces in another corner. The sound of groaning could be heard from the echoes of the dungeon. And to top it all off there was no window and it was very dark.

Nat was eager to escape, by pushing the door, but to no avail. The man laughed while he was lying down without a care in the world and said: “You are eager,”

Nat gave him a snare, did not reply and continued to push the door.

“Good job in taking those guards out!” said the man.

Nat looked at him and asked: “Are you him?”

“Ummm... and who are you referring to?” asked the man.

“You have the same type of ring my father has,” replied Nat,” Can you please explain? What are you talking about?” said the man

“Infinity? Are you Infinity?” replied Nat.

The man was silent for a moment and said in a slow serious tone: “Yes. Yes, I am,”

“So you’re the one supposed to save the Multi-verse? You can’t even save yourself from this King! You don’t even have your sanity!” anguished Nat.

“You’re quite pushy, aren’t you?” said Infinity.

He laughed and started singing *crazy-gnarls Barkley* whilst Nat was trying to answer the questions in the song.

After another few moments, Infinity broke the silence and said: "So you're a dimensions hopper?"

"I am now," replied Nat in a sarcastic tone:

"So you say your father sent you for me?" asked Infinity.

Nat replied in a dry tone: "Ya".

"What's his name", asked Infinity.

Nat replied: "James ...,"

She was cut off abruptly by Infinity who cried out: "Woah, Woah, Woah, Woah! Don't you know you should never name someone by their real name in the Multi-verse?"

"No but my father did say you would explain everything," replied Nat.

Infinity sighed and grunted: "It's because it's going to put a giant target on that person's back, since in the Multi-verse you can make an awful lot of enemies. Enemies that want you dead, even before you born and they don't play by the books!! So they attack your family or yourself at your weakest, which is basically when your baby,"

"So how are you supposed to help my father?" asked Nat.

Infinity replied: "I still don't know who your father is dear,"

Nat groaned.

"Rest for tomorrow. We are going to escape," Infinity said to Nat.

Nat slept for a solid 5 hours, when some singing woke her up. It was Infinity and he was singing *Wolves-Rag'n'Bone*and she looked beyond the bars of the door and saw a creature resembling a large wolf, completely black with red glowing eyes and sharp teeth. It started running towards the door. Nat flew back as it bashed into the door and luckily it didn't get in. The sound of screaming could be heard. Nat could see the creature's paws from under the door as it was scratching on it but left when the song finished. She looked out the door and saw no one there anymore except for the remains of the soldier's corpses.

"What was that? Was that the creature killing those guards?" Nat asked in horror.

"You don't know how to use that ring still, do you?" replied Infinity.

Nat shook her head.

"These rings can open portals, make constructs and translators, and act as life-supports etc... They basically can do miracles, but at a cost. Songs help reduce the cost or help to pay the bill, if you will," continued Infinity.

Nat looked at her ring.

"Why songs?" asked Nat in bewilderment.

"Because all people will hear it, but those who matter will listen to it," replied Infinity propehtically.

"Go back to sleep. It's going to be a big day tomorrow,"

V. Freedom

Nat was woken up by Infinity. It was around 8 o'clock and it was dead silent.

"Can you blast open the door, please?" he asked,"How?" Nat asked.

He replied: "Aim your hand at the place you want to target. Make a fist and then squeeze that fist. I would do it myself but I need to store the power for later," replied Infinity.

Nat did so but nothing happened. She looked sheepishly at Infinity.

Infinity said: "Oh yeah, you have to also think about shooting an energy blast. As they say, 'Thinking is a hobby'.

Nat did so and blew open the door and it flew a few feet away.

They ran out and Infinity shouted: "Okay let's scramble out of here but before we leave, let's free the people," And so they did.

Most of the prisoners held in the dungeons were charged for standing up for their rights and not giving all of their possessions to the Kingdom.

After all the prisoners were freed, Nat blew open another hole through the wall, forgetting there was a moat surrounding the dank subterranean dungeons. The cells quickly began to flood with water ..... and alligators.

Infinity gave Nat an anguished look and proceeded to wrestle down an alligator with his ring and yelled to everyone to run up the stairs and out the main door.

"But the guards will kill us, we will have no hope of surviving!" the prisoners yelled back.

Infinity glanced at Nat and the alligator and back to Nat and smiled and said: "Oh yes you will".

They all proceeded to go up the stairs with Infinity in the front holding the large alligator. Infinity opened the door threw the alligator outside, slamming the door shut again. After a few seconds, screams could be heard outside with men shouting "There is alligator in the hall" and "Run, run". The guards rushed back, trying to battle the alligator. Then suddenly both Nat and Infinity kicked open the door and started shooting blasts of energy with their rings slaughtering the guards "So are we going to take on the King now?" asked Nat.

Infinity replied: "No we're not the ones going to take him on. Let's get these people out first. Quick slice that rope!" shouted back Infinity.

Nat obeyed and cut the rope and the drawbridge fell down. They all escaped safely. The same could not be said for the guard "So what now?" asked Nat breathlessly.

Infinity commanded the prisoners to gather as many people they could find and watched them scatter in all directions.

Infinity looked at Nat and said with a French accents: "Vive la Révolution!"

A chorus of "Gather, gather our Savior is here" could be heard as people started rushing at the gates. The King went to the castle walls and saw the mob of protesters growing like a tidal wave. He ran back into his castle's Great Hall and ordered all of his guards to take a defensive formation and protect him.

A few moments later, almost all the town was there. About 500 people. Infinity climbed up onto a boulder and broke out in song *Freedom-Pharrell Williams*. hyping the masses and instilling into them the required revolutionary spirit. As the song finished they all charged into the castle and the guards began shooting volleys of arrows, that sadly managed to pierce and fell a number of those people.

But the crowd continued rushing to the throbs of *Megalovnia-Undertale*. No doubt courtesy of Infinity. The Mob felt its power. The old felt young, the poor felt rich, the young felt strong, the sick felt healthy. With a rage compared to the berserkers, they charged into the castle, taking on every guard in their way. Even Nat felt the overwhelming thirst for blood. The guards stood no chance. Like flies swarming into a bug zapper, their death was inevitable and soon Infinity was standing upon the King.

"So what are you waiting for? Just get it over with!" snarled the King.

Infinity looked at him with disgust and said: "That is not up to me. It's up to them,"

He stood aside letting the people get to him.

The screams of the King could be heard. Finally, the people got their 'rights'.

"Okay let's go to a safe place, so we can talk and have a bite. Go ahead open up the portal," Infinity said to Nat.

"How?" asked Nat.

"Simple!! It's just like shooting. Point at a wall or into the air. It's mentally connected to you. Think of where you want to go to or which dimension you want to arrive at, then just squeeze your fist," replied Infinity

Nat thought of the street off F.R.I.E.N.D.S café and opened the portal and they both went through it, as it closed behind them again.

VI. Training level

As Nat and Infinity passed through the portal, they came out onto the street in front of the café. Nobody noticed their portal. They went inside the café, passing a few familiar faces coming out prior to their going in. Infinity jumped on the couch in the middle from the back and sat on it and Nat sat on the armchair to the left. Nat caught everyone's attention at the café with her torn clothes.

“You’ve got good taste. I’m surprised people your age still watch this show,” Infinity remarked.

Nat smiled.

“Seriously how old are you 25? 26?” asked Infinity.

“I’m under 24,” replied Nat.

Infinity shocked said: “What kind of idiot would send someone under 24 into the Multi-verse and not even explain a bit about anything. You could seriously yourself hurt!” said Infinity in shock.

Nat gave Infinity a look and asked: “Why were you there?”

“Oh, I was just training,” replied Infinity.

Nat said with a laugh: “You call that training? You’re one strange man, Infinity!” Nat cried out laughingly.

Infinity started to sing *Feel it still-Portugal. The Man*

The waiter came and asked: Hi guys. What can I get for you?

“I’ll have a Cappuccino please and she will have a….,” Infinity replied.

“ An Espresso, please,” Nat replied.

The waiter took the order and left.

“So what’s going to happen to them?” asked Nat.

"Anything actually. It all depends on them, how they decide to live their lives. That is their story now,"

"So about my father. He gave me this and told me to give it to you," said Nat

Nat handed the projector pen to Infinity.

Infinity went up to the bar and said: "We will have it 'To Go', please,"

He proceeded to pay for the coffees and took them.

"Let's go somewhere with fewer people," Infinity told Nat.

Infinity opened up a portal into an empty field and then passed the Espresso to Nat.

Infinity quizzingly asked Nat "Tell me why you need my help? And how do you know me?" "My father, he told me you were his teacher. His friend," Nat replied.

"Bullshit! I was never a teacher. Well accept a few times... but not in this matter,"

"And as for your help," continued Nat "my father told me you could take on Key. He's about to destroy my dimension. My father told me you were the only hope of defeating him,"

"I think your father has mistaken me for someone else. Do you know how powerful Key is?" Infinity replied.

"No, no I'm pretty sure it is you. My father said he would be the strongest and most powerful person there, with the name of Infinity. This is no coincidence!" insisted Nat.

"I'm not the person you are looking for. The only thing that comes with me is pain and tragedy,"

He then proceeded to sing*Boulevard of Broken Dreams - Green Day* very emotionally.

“Well, I’m willing to walk with you but please help me save my universe,” begged Nat.

“Okay, I will help you but you’ve got to understand…,” replied Infinity.

Infinity then proceeded to break into song*Hometown – Twenty One Pilots*

“I completely understand and agree to those terms,” replied Nat.

Infinity replied in a jokingly manner: “These new terms and conditions are literally everywhere,”

“What?” asked Nat.

“Oh nothing, it's just some inside joke that you won’t understand,” replied Infinity.

Nat replied with an awkward smile: Okay then. Can you please stop with the singing it’s getting annoying,”

Infinity replied: “If you’re with me, the singing stays. That is final!” replied Infinity.

“Can you give me a minute please, the pen has written private and that reminds me to scramble the watchers,” Infinity suddenly exclaimed.

”The what?” asked Nat.

“The watchers. We are in the Multi-verse, so people are bound to be watching us. It could be by reading, seeing, hearing, etc… What I’m doing is making it harder for them to see what’s happening and stop them from figuring out stuff that is important that I don’t want them to know! The one I’m about to activate isn’t that hard to breach but some get really difficult. You would have to search all Time and Space and Dimensions to figure it out. Some of them are even in plain sight but some are with hidden keys that need to be decoded.

Infinity’s ring then announced “15 minutes encoding activated in 3… 2… 1…”

fdnjiudjhjjjknhjkhjhjxhhjkhnkjnjkgnjkbflnbl;pxdmehjx[‘thj[‘xjbj[‘tribjjx[;h [;xtn[pnhofhn[x’yn[‘xokjy’[]kxy[jk[xyjkkj;xkfy’jkmxfgkhfgetxkjjfojkopjkofk jjkokyjokyjkpojkokj[pjkooutopkjokj[kjkkjkhokherekoyokyopkxyoj

VII. The Message

so she could become greater than we could ever be. You already met our son. Well one of them. Glad to say they both have humanity, they have a conscience. Not like our counterpart. One of our sons is out exploring but the other one I'll give him the choice but it will be his choice. He will most likely not accept it as he has his own family now. But take care of the ones that we have in our care.

You later have to find Joy and Rust. You already have Centinus with you. Remember there is power in numbers but only if the people are worthy.

James laughed and said: "You remember when we were children. We were always saying 'Why does everything have a happy ending' but now we keep asking ourselves 'what happened to those happy endings?' Please don't let this be a bad ending."

James dragged his hands through his hair and continued: "Nat has high expectations from you now. I kind of hyped you up a bit too much. So if you're going to let her down, do it slowly. Do remember though when people asked you to do the impossible you always laughed and did it. It wasn't always fun but you did it nevertheless. Hero Key out."

The projection faded out and the video stopped. Tears were coming down Infinity's face.

Infinity broke the projection pen and sent it to some unknown star. Infinity wiped off the tears from his face and went back to Nat.

"Okay. I'll help you but your father told me to teach you some things first," said Infinity

"What things?" asked Nat.

"Some life lessons. Things you have to know if you going to be out in the Multi-verse," replied Infinity.

"Forget that!! My whole dimension is in danger!!" snapped back Nat.

Walk on Water-Eminem ft.Beyonce

Rujrep[9tup0hateg[wy[9u5=4yvm45]yeit]hig]bm]eimvh0timh]0ukeyumimh]m0mv[iycvm450yim]0vi,]wiy,]0l5i4yvm],5[y,i40im0bm]y[vi[0yiv]054iyoui460iv0i50ib-ium]-vm,i]-45,iyv4ibm]-bi]4v]5lljuto;tltltu;y;y;tjj

VIII. The Base

"I don't need any superhuman powers. I just need someone that can help me," said Nat.

Infinity kindly smiled at her and said: "Let's go to my base. Believe me, you need some upgrades for where we are going to go search for him," So where is your base? Where do you live?" asked Nat.

"Me? I live with my friend and as to where it is, it's a starship outside of time and space. Between the spaces of every dimension in the Multi-verse. It is a very hard place to get to. That's why I chose it to be there," replied Infinity.

"Wait a minute your base is between dimensions? How's that possible? I thought they were just timelines in that space!" exclaimed Nat.

"Well no. It's actually space there. You see, the Multiverse is even in the other space named the Multi-Multiverse. Because the Multi-verse has dimension hoppers and they become outside forces effecting the Multi-verse. As a result of that, the Multi-verse itself acts like a dimension and this goes on and on until infinity. The only thing they have in common is dimension zero. You must've read about it, since these portals are using it to go to other dimensions," explained Infinity.

"Oh yes! I took a course whilst in University. It just didn't know, you could've stopped between the spaces, replied Nat.

"Yup! That was a really hard task to do! The way I did it was to vibrate faster than the speed of light. Then I opened the portal through it," said Infinity, with a hint of pride.

"How did you manage not to turn into energy then?"

"One, I wasn't the one going at that speed. Two, there are loopholes all around!"

"Okay, then how are we supposed to go there?"

"It's on Portal Lock," Infinity replied.

"Meaning?" asked Nat.

"Only some portal openers can open it. Here, let me give you the key. Give me your hand.

Nat gave her left hand with the ring, as Infinity took his right hand and made a fist. Nat seeing what Infinity did, also made a fist as well. They put both their fists together as in a bro-fist and then Infinity commanded: "Give Portal Key Purgatory!"

"This ring already has the key," chimed the ring.

"It's your father's ring isn't?" asked Infinity.

"Yes it is," replied Nat.

"Then know how much he loves you, because he gave you all of his secrets. Basically, every dimension can be accessed using his ring," said Infinity

"I'm guessing you don't know how to access it though. Some dimension hoppers put codes, names, songs or words first, but the person that owns that dimension, must first give the key to someone, like how we were doing it. You then say the name, access code, song whatever, and hey presto a portal will open, leading to the chosen destination. Normally the portal is no more than a few meters away from you. It can also be accessed by vibrating through all the dimensions but that would be crazy and needlessly dangerous! Because normally the dimension hoppers put up defenses for any intruders! You already have the key. The portal can be accessed by singing the song 'Dream'," said Infinity.

"Oh so that's why you chose the space between spaces in the Multi-verse, as it is harder for people to get there!" replied Nat.

"Exactly! Bravo! Now should I do the honors or do you want to?" asked Infinity.

"Go ahead I'm not much of a singer," replied Nat.

"Okay then but do know I'm not much of a singer either! The ring makes it sound good. It mentally projects the song into the listener's head, making it sound like the exact song sung by its artist!" said Infinity.

Infinity then started singing *Dream-imagine Dragon*and a portal opened up. They both went through it after the song finished. Infinity felt very sad and emotional after the song. Once they went through and came out to the entrance platform Infinity said: "Welcome to my home, sweet home, Purgatory! Do make yourself at home, "Why Purgatory?" asked Nat.

"It's a long story, filled with very bad memories. I do not want to talk about it now, if you don't mind," replied Infinity.

"Sorry I asked!" said Nat

"It's okay. Sorry for bursting out. You must be tired. Now follow me so I can find you a nice room," said Infinity.

"How many rooms does this place have?" asked Nat

"28 bedrooms and over 500 different rooms, halls and what-nots" replied Infinity.

"Wow!! It's a really big place!" exclaimed Nat.

"Yeah there's a lot of emptiness in the space between dimensions. Might as well use it generously," said Infinity.

Infinity's ring began to beep. Infinity brought his hand up and it projected a screen. It was a holographic call. Infinity started talking to that person. Nat couldn't make out what those two were saying but she could hear "Welcome back" and "Who is she?" As the call finished, Nat asked: "Was that your friend that you were talking about?"

"Yes. Something has come up. Can I take you to the living room and then you can go to your new room?" said Infinity.

"No rush," said Nat.

They both started walking through a long hall. Nat looked out the window of the hall and witnessed dimension upon dimension as she walked down the corridor. As she stopped to look at them the dimensions stopped changing, like the frames of a film.

"Wow!! This is so beautiful! Why is it doing this?" asked Nat.

Infinity stood and looked out with Nat and replied: "What you're seeing is the Multi-verse. The Multi-verse is like a rope. It's built by numerous strands woven together and since you have a 3 dimensional body, you're observing everything frame by frame, so when you're moving it's constantly changing because you're looking at another dimension. It's a very cool effect but you can only see if you're in the space between dimensions in the Multi-verse. Now if you had a 4 dimensional body you would have seen all of its time at once and if he had a 5 dimensional body you will see it as a rope, as a collection of individual strands with electric looking currents going through them,"

Nat was stunned by how beautiful it was.

They both proceeded to walk into the living room. It took about 10 minutes to reach it. The living room was a huge room with a giant curved TV on the wall, like a cinema screen, with an enormous multi-storied library surrounding the room behind them. In the center, close to the TV, was a curved couch with a couple adjacent armchairs. Behind the couch was a small bar with a window behind it looking onto the Multi-verse.

"Can I get you anything? There's a bar right there. You could literally have any food from the Multi-verse," offered Infinity.

"I would die for a burger right now!!" exclaimed Nat.

Infinity went to get the burger from the Multi-versal food maker (also known as a "Multi-receivable Oven, which is an oven into which any food requested from any dimension is transported into the Oven.

While Infinity was bringing the burger, Nat asked: "Have you read all these books? Must have taken over 500 years!"

Infinity gave her the burger and said: "754 years to be precise! I have even classified them by genre. One-third of them are actually comic books. From all over the Multi-verse. Some are even about me!"

Nat, almost choking on her burger, exclaimed: "What? 754 years? You've got to be joking! How old are you?"

"I don't know to be honest. I lost count after 935 googolplex human earth years. It was becoming a hassle trying to remember,"

"So how have you managed to stay alive for so long?" asked Nat.

"I make clones, without a consciousness, of course, of myself and transfer my own consciousness into that new clone. I can also make the clone look like anyone or any species I want. Basically, all dimension hoppers can do this. But something that is very rare for us is our original body. If we ever decide to go back to our original universe, we go back to her using our original body and that will be our last life,"

Nat asked: "Well how do you know that is you? How do you know that if you are the original and if the original you would have done something else? How do you know that the body is the original and you are not the mind?

"To be honest we don't know but it is the best thing we could have done. It's that or immortality and living forever would be painful mentally. For those that normally do live forever are sad. I should know I basically am living forever,"

"Are you certain that you are not afraid of dying?" asked Nat.

"No not at all. A lot of people think death is a bad thing. It's not. Life-and-death are two sides of the same coin. You cannot have one without the other or else they will both be meaningless. Death without Life is nothing. For nothing has become; and Life with no Death is similarly meaningless because after a while your purpose has no meaning," replied Infinity.

"So what's the point? What's the meaning of life?" pondered Nat.

Infinity replied: "That is not up for me to say to you. But after all these years of experience, one can say is that Life has no meaning, no story, no point. It is you that gives it meaning. You give it its storyline, you give it its point. Since in the Multi-verse everything is happening, don't let that stop you from doing what you want to do or what you think is the right thing to do. But don't just go around and do some stupid shit and using this as your excuse. You still have your own morals and values. Your own conscience and notion of right or wrong. Don't allow the monster in you to ever come out. If you let it come out, you are no better than a bag full of excrement thrown at a windshield of a car..

Nat chuckled and exclaimed: "No need to go all philosophical on me!"

"If you will excuse me, I'll be right back. My friend is waiting for me. If you want, there is a remote you can turn on the TV. Enjoy it! It's Multiversal Wide. I recommend the Dead Pool Series," Said Infinity.

"No worries. Thanks!" said Nat.

Infinity left leaving Nat to eat her burger in peace. She picked up the remote and turned on the TV.

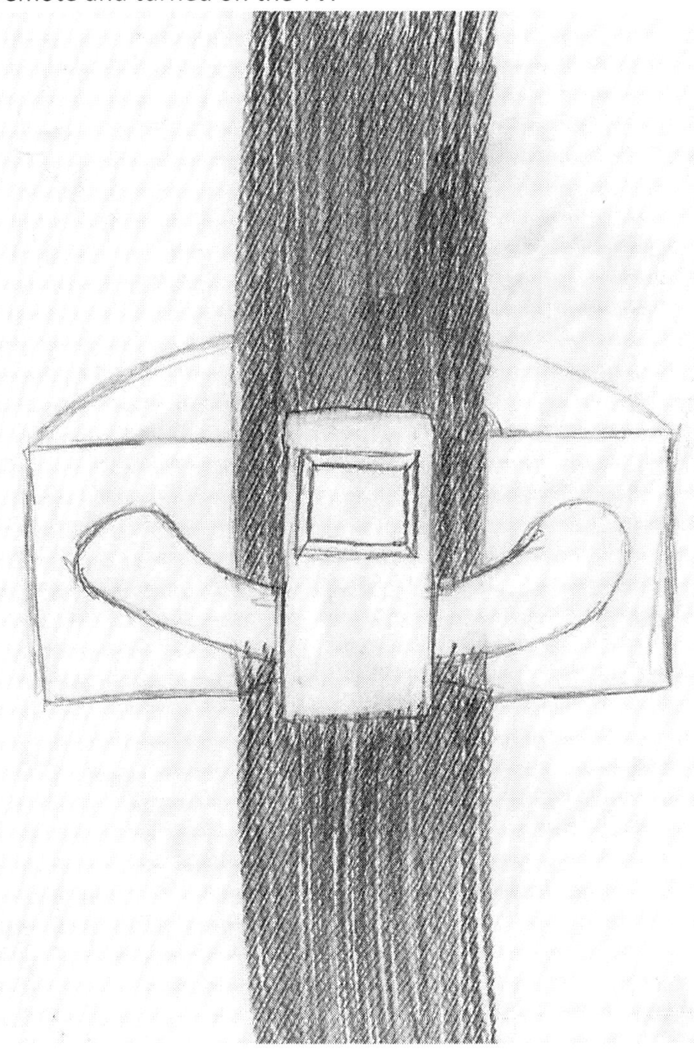

IX.Upgrade

Quite a number of minutes had passed before Infinity returned. Nat was watching the animated DeadPool series and she was enjoying it very much.

"Wow! This show is really good. It's a shame that it got canceled in my dimension," said Nat

Infinity smiled and absently said: "Yeah. Are you ready to go?"

"Yes!" said Nat.

"Great! Just on the way, let's change your clothes. I don't think that torn dress is very comfortable!" replied Infinity.

"Thank you. That will be very much appreciated!" said Nat.

They both started walking down yet another hall.

"So how long is this thing?" asked Nat.

"It actually loops around. This place actually goes around the Multi-verse!" replied Infinity.

"Cool... cool," said Nat.

After a few moments of silence, Infinity said: "My friend and I were talking and we decided to give you an upgrade and some new tech!"

"Oh like the James Bond kind of upgrades and tech, huh?" said Nat excitedly.

"Yes if you look at it that way. I am quite shocked that James Bond is still quite a thing," said Infinity.

They both laughed and continued walking down the hall.

They stopped at a door in the middle of the hallway. It was password protected. Infinity entered in the password ########. The door opened, as did a few subsequent vaults. The door first led into a trophy room. Nat could see many famous items there. She was thrilled out of her mind. They continued on to another corridor, passing a battery of other rooms.

“Why was that door locked?” asked Nat.

"This part of my base is more important than the other half!” explained Infinity.

“Why?” asked Nat.

“Well, I keep all my valuables on this side,” replied Infinity.

They finally reached a largish room filled with all sorts of gadgets, hanging either on the walls , floating in air or adorning mannequins,"And my lady, we have arrived!” exclaimed Infinity.

Nat stood and looked around the room,” Quick question, do you have a tech implant?” asked Infinity matter of fact.

“Oh yes. My father recently released it to the public,” said Nat.

“Great. That simplifies things immensely,” said Infinity, noticeably relieved

Infinity proceeded to gently touch Nat behind her neck with his index and middle fingers, where the implant was located, simultaneously looking around the room at the various objects.

“Okay then. You should now have access to them,” he said.

They proceeded to walk to a mannequin dressed in a glowing skintight white suit, embossed with a golden key in the middle of the chest, “This is a symbiotic morphing Pico suit, or as they say in English, a Pico tech photonic suit, which sticks to the host, morphing into whatever clothes or uniform the host wants it to be. So if you want to change your clothes, you just got to go into the menu in your implant to change it.

You can even access it by only thinking about it. It also has a useful feature in being thermal adaptive. So you'll never be annoyed by the temperature. It is also shockproof and to a point bulletproof. It also has the ability to make shields for protection, swords and it can also generate protonic blasts or lasers and anything in between. Furthermore it can glow in its default mode, which can cause an intense glowing, temporarily blinding your opponents. Lastly, it keeps itself and the host clean. Please just don't use it inside the base. And take care of it because it's rather rare. Its Key tech, you know," explained Infinity.

"What, Key make this?" asked Nat.

"Yes and no. But not the Key you are thinking about. There used to be a whole Empire of them. The one who made this was actually a decent person but yes the Key destroying the dimensions, is also using this. He just puts it in reverse mode. It can also take care of your wounds. Put your hand on the mannequin. The way you get it off, is by singing the song dress. Whoever is touching the clothes, while the owner is singing the song, will be transferred onto them and if you don't touch someone, you have to touch any surface and the clothes will be put on that. Any questions?" replied Nat wearily.

"Yes, only few, if you don't mind. One, are you wearing one? Two, what do you mean by putting it in reverse mode? Three, can you sing the song? I am afraid I do not know it!" said Nat exasperatedly.

"Yes I'm wearing one and you set the option to 'Drain Light'instead of giving it out. It really annoys the eyes after a long exposure. Sure, I will sing it. Put your hand on the suit," replied Infinity. Infinity proceeded to sing *Dress-Taylor Swift*and the suit, in liquid form, started flowing and moving on to Nat's hand, then up her arm and body. Momentarily it had completely encapsulated her. Nat thought of her old clothes and the suit morphed into them.

"You're kidding! After all this effort, this is the best you can do? Have a sense of style, girl! You can do much better than that! Remember cost is not a factor here" cringed Infinity.

Nat paused for a moment and thought back to a memory of a stylish yet practical Issey Miyake outfit that had taken her fancy in a boutique window some months ago, without any consideration of her pocket. The clothes momentarily morphed into a pleated black leather-laced jacket, tight grey polo-neck and skin-tight trousers, flared at the bottom.

"Now that's more like it," said Infinity approvingly.

He then handed Nat her phone.

Nat glared at him and said in an angry tone: "You've had this all this time? I was worried sick about it. Why didn't you give it to me earlier?"

"Well my dear, you have didn't have any pockets! So I could give it to you at that time. Now you do!" said Infinity patiently.

Nat gave Infinity a sheepish look, knowing he was right. They moved on to a table with a necklace with a smooth oval pendant displayed on it.

"Okay then. You see this nifty necklace? Well it makes a photonic force field around the wearer. Since you're using your original body and the suit doesn't provide sufficient protection, I recommend you wear it at all times. It can stop any type of bullet, laser, projectile, etc... It can also make a safe haven, as in not allowing people that you don't want to get too close to you. It will burn them. Do note though, that it is not fully impenetrable. If something breaks through the shield, it will get through but that is a hard task to accomplish!" said Infinity.

Nat eagerly picked the necklace up and put it on over her head.

"I love it! Thank you!" said Nat gleefully.

"Your welcome but we're not quite done yet," said Infinity.

He then picked up a box containing two lenses and gave them to Nat.

"Put them on. These are 'Smart Lenses'. They allow you to enhance or see farther by squinting your eyes. You can also change the way you see by opening your eyes as wide as you can and then closing them. This way, you can activate night vision, infrared, ultraviolet, radio waves, etc.. If your eyes are weak, it can help you immensely. It also has a profiling program, which analyzes and tells you everything about the object you are viewing. Oh, you can also change your eye color if that's your fancy," said Infinity.

They started walking again. Nat tried to test the lenses out, stumbled and was lost in the number of viewing modes to which it could be changed. This caught Infinity's intention, "Just think of your normal vision," he said reassuringly.

Nat's vision refocused back to normal. Infinity took a grey leather satchel off the wall and gave it to Nat.

"You've heard of the saying 'Don't judge a peppercorn by its size'? Well this satchel is a 'Dimensional Satchel, meaning you can store anything inside of it,. It has almost infinite space, limited only by the dimensions of the satchel. If you want to retrieve anything, which you have already stored in it, there's a soft AI inside of it. The AI will hand you it, when you put your hand in it and also store it for you. I've put a food maker inside of it already with a selection of all menus in the Multi-verse palatable to Humans. You never know when you'll get hungry! Our rings can actually do this but since you don't know how to use it yet, I'm giving you this for now, until you learn," said Infinity.

They continued walking forward and until Infinity suddenly took a pen-ish looking device from a table and threw it to Nat. Nat caught it in the air. Infinity explained: "That is a portable fusion, wireless generator so you can keep your devices charged at all times!"

At the end of the room Infinity took a key with a button in the middle on it. Infinity remarked: "This is the key to your room. You can access it from anywhere in the Multiverse. Aportal will open leading you to your room. Okay then let's head to your room!

Nat and Infinity started walking again. Infinity paused and stopped at the medical hall.

"Quickly get on the table and lay down. I'm going to insert a device that will stop you from having a stomach-ache ever again,"

"Why though? Can't I just use the bathroom?" said Nat in disbelief.

"In some dimensions, there are no bathrooms! Or none that you would care to use!! This is basically a portable bathroom, which is located inside your Large Intestines!" replied Infinity.

"Okay then, you have a valid point there!" said Nat approvingly, remembering her OCD for sparkling clean toilets.

Nat lay down and the device scanned her, "All done! I also upgraded your health bots to protect you against all known illnesses and viruses,"

"How did you do it that fast?" said Nat in amazement.

Infinity laughed and said: "Out of all these devices this is the only thing that caught your attention?"

They both started laughing. They continued walking until they reached a smaller hall and continued a bit more until they reached Nat's room.

"Here's your room. It is equipped with all the things that you may need. It has a bathroom as well with really good water pressure, if you want to shower".

Nat went inside her room and turned around, "Thank you" she said to Infinity, with emotion.

"You're welcome, my dear. I'm going to go take a shower and then I will make a list of all the possible places he could be, with my friend. In the meanwhile relax it is going to be a long trip. See you In a few hours. My room is at the end of the hall. Knock on it. If I'm there I will come out. If not continue going down the hall until the end the last door on your right. See it? That is my friend's room, in the control room.

Infinity then left the room. As he was walking down the hallway towards his own room he could hear the song *Dress – Taylor Swift* coming from Nat's room.

X. The Search Commences

After Infinity took his shower, he dressed into a fresh set of clothes and went to the last room on the right at the end of the hall. The room was filled with a bank of monitors. Some of the monitors showed camera views inside the base somewhere. Some showed the view through people's eyes. The room was very high-tech. In the room, there was a single tall swivel chair. He started talking with his friend.

"I have to find him," said Infinity.

"And whom is him exactly?" His friend replied.

"You know bloody well whom I'm talking about," replied Infinity.

"Why must you humans be so stupid? I'm not going to help you with your suicide mission. I am glad you're playing with others again but not to this point!" the friend exclaimed, noticeably exasperated.

"I wouldn't be doing this for anyone else, except for her. She is special," said Infinity defensively.

"Everyone is 'special' to you, so what makes her so different?" said with the friend with a snide laugh.

Infinity didn't reply verbally but transmitted a telepathic message to his friend.

The friend sighed and exclaimed: "God damn simians!! Fine! I shall help you. Do you have any leads?"

"Not yet but I can get some from the Multi-verse," said Infinity.

Thereupon, Infinity broke into song again, singing*Secrets-One Republic*. He started transmitting his newly song-provided leads to his friend telepathically.

"Can you organize them by least probable to most probable, please? I want to teach Nat some things before finding him," said Infinity.

His friend replied in a smirk-ish tone: "You do know I don't know where he is, right! You *do* know he is one of the hardest people to find!!! ... ... I'll try my best,"

"Thank you, my friend. IOU big time!" said Infinity

A few hours had passed before Nat came into the room, finding Infinity sitting in the chair, apparently waiting for her," Any luck?" she asked in a concerned tone.

"Not yet. I'm still waiting on my friend to make the probability list," answered Infinity.

Thereupon his friend sent him a mental message saying: "It was completed four hours ago,"

"Then why didn't you send it before? What's with the coy business?" said a bewildered Infinity.

"Because I wanted to make an impression upon her!" his friend telepathically replied.

His friend proceeded to send him the list. Infinity quickly checked the list by projecting it with his Ring.

Infinity started reading the list aloud saying: "So we are starting off with the Utopia based dimension,"

"Why would he be in the Utopia dimension?"

"One reason, it was on your algorithm. Two, he most probably wants to destroy it. Don't worry though. Even if he's not there, you will have a good time and learn something," Infinity replied, adding as an afterthought "That is, if he isn't there. Otherwise not so much!"

Infinity, seeing Nat was very worried, after saying that, sang *California girls – Katy Perry* while morphing his clothes to look as if he was wearing a bikini. He started dancing a silly dance while singing.

His friend messaged him saying: “What on Earth are you doing now. You look as if you are in that episode of The Simpsons, the one in which Homer is dancing!”

Nat started chuckling. After the song was finished, Infinity morphed his clothes back to his regular attire and he opened a portal, saying: “Whenever you’re ready, then,”

“I’m ready but who were you talking to? There is no one here beside me!

“Wonderful!! Now she thinks I am crazier than I actually am! Bye, thank you for the help!”

Infinity’s friend messaged him “:-) byeeeee,”

Nat and Infinity walked through the portal into the great unknown and portal closed behind them.

XI. Utopia

A portal open and Nat and Infinity stepped out. The instance they came out, they both felt completely elated. The air was so fresh and clean. The temperature was so perfect. The lighting was always correct. There were no flaws to be made out. In the distance, there was a very advanced city. Just being there was more relaxing than staying for a year in the best 10-star hotel in their own dimension.

Nat, in a relaxed tone, lazily asked: “So how are we supposed to find him?”

“He is someone who is drawn to commotion. We just have to do something to get his attention. But first, do you want to enjoy this dimension a bit?” said Infinity.

“Okay. It won’t hurt to have a little break,” said Nat.

They both proceeded to amble laconically towards the city. The city was next to a beach. The people in the city were all happily going about their way, without a care in the world. It was just so blissful! They noticed everything was controlled by automatons and all the humans were having the time of their lives. They both went into a resort and started enjoying the amenities of the dimension. To blend in, they morphed their clothes into casual summer attire.

After 16 hours at the spa, Nat absently asked: “How long has it been?”

“16 hours, 25 minutes, 12 seconds,” Infinity precisely replied.

“Hasn’t really been that long, has it?” Nat asked with surprise.

”Time flies fast when you’re having fun!” yawned Infinity.

After a few joyful moments, Infinity spoke again: "Did you know, that this dimension has never experienced a bad thing. Everything was just here in the beginning -- perfectly.

"No. I can't say I knew that'" said Nat.

After a few more soothing minutes, Infinity asked: "Don't you feel anything missing?"

"Nope. Everything's perfect. Why do you ask?" Nat replied.

"Well you see, because this world never experienced anything bad or evil, after a while it will start getting boring. The people here also lack freedom of thought. They're always in this state where everything is handed to them. They don't think for themselves and because of this they have never done anything for themselves,"

"Ah huh. Then why is not affecting me or you?" replied Nat.

"Actually it is. I have experience in how to handle it. You, on the other hand, don't. Even the way you are speaking is changing. After spending an extended period of time here. Start noticing that it begins to get a tad dull and stale. Because just like life-and-death, Good and Evil are two sides of the same coin.

They both have to exist. If you want to experience them fully and separately, it is necessary that they both exist. If only Evil existed, you would have nothing but a bad time, misery, anger, pain and anguish. If only Goodness existed, it would be, well, a place like this. A place, where everyone would be sluggish and trance-like. After a while, it will become boring because you have nothing else to compare it to. After a while, Good will transgress into a form of Evil. People think this place is be amazing but they don't look at the full picture. When you get back to a normal living state, it will be much harder. The higher you're high, the lower, your lows shall be. Good and Evil...It's this beautiful story, you know that will never end," Infinity pronounced.

After a few more moments, Infinity stretched and stood up and said: "Okay, let's get going and searching for him!"

“Oh no! A few more minutes, please,” pleaded Nat.

No! That’s the elation talking,” Infinity replied firmly.

Nat groaned and Infinity started singing *Chained to the Rhythm - Katy Perry* and started doing everything that the song sang about. People all around Infinity started awakening from their trance-like existence, realizing the fallacy of the world they were living in. Nat too awoke from her trance.

Nat, numbed with a dull headache, of the sort one gets from sleeping too much, tied to focus and said: “How do we find him now?”

“We wait a few minutes. It is usually fast. In the meantime, I will open up the portal for the next world,” replied Infinity.

“What will happen to the people?” asked Nat.

“Life!” pronounced Infinity.

After a few moments, Infinity disappointedly said: “It doesn’t look like he’s coming. Let’s go to the next world,”

Infinity and Nat stepped through the already open portal. They came out onto a drab street in a shabby neighborhood. They both felt this intense low. Infinity started singing *Lost in Paradise-Rihanna* and their depression got better but only somewhat. Infinity dealt with the low better than Nat.

“What did that song do just now? Does it always feel so bad after leaving these dimensions?” Nat asked.

“That song helps with lows and dampens the memory, so you won’t get addicted to it. You can have good times without being in Utopia. Yes, it also was this intense for me, the first time. That’s why I never go to those dimensions, unless I'm forced to,” replied Infinity sympathetically.

XII. The Dying World

Infinity spoke into his ring, activating the spectator mode. He then said the same to Nat's ring.

"Why did you activate this mode?" she asked.

"Because we need a few minutes," Infinity replied.

"So where are we? This place looks familiar enough!" Nat asked.

"Well this is your normal, run-of-mill dimension. There is nothing special about it. Except for its planet is dying, all life forms actually. Not just the planet but it's starting from the earth.

"What's starting?" she asked.

"The Necromace virus'" Infinity replied.

"The Zombie virus? There are no zombies here, though. It's just a normal neighborhood with kids!" a visibly startled Nat exclaimed, "You see that kid over there with the cough mask. He's infected. I would give him around 5 more days, tops," replied Infinity.

"Are we in danger of being infected then?" Nat asked with concern.

"No. Our health bots prevent that. We're in the clear," said Infinity.

""So why can't we help them? Why can't we cure them?" said Nat, rather relieved and now in Good Samaritan mode.

"Unfortunately, it's much too late for that," Infinity said.

Suddenly a huge explosion occurred, together with its telltale mushroom cloud. Destroying and evaporating miles and miles away. Nat fell on her knees at the shock of what she had just witnessed.

"We could've saved them," said Nat quietly.

"No, we couldn't. If we came out of spectator mode, we would have died along with them. I showed you this so you learn that you can't always save everyone. Some people go through their whole lives thinking they can. They normally end up being sad. Living will be hard for them because you can't give pity to everyone. I don't want you to be numbed by this sort of things and at the same time I don't want you to feel as if it was your fault. Many people in this Multi-verse think they owe their lives to everyone. This is not the case. You don't owe anyone anything. So don't blame yourself for matters that you cannot prevent, "Infinity replied.

Infinity laughed out loud and continued saying: "There are actually some dimension hoppers in the Multi-verse that try to save everyone. Some of them inadvertently even manage spread to the diseases to other dimensions. Ironic isn't it. After a time, they got fewer and fewer, until you can't find them anymore these days. They still exist but they're rare. I guess they started accepting the inevitable truth,"

Infinity held out his hand and helped Nat get up. He began to fly straight up to the sky and into to Space, dragging Nat with him, at noticeably fast speed.

"You can fly? You can fly!" exclaimed Nat, with the bewilderment of a child.

"Yes! So can you. I'll teach you a little later," said Infinity, hurtling towards Space, escaping the radiation blast.

"Why are you going up towards Space? We cannot breathe there!!" cautioned Nat in panic.

Infinity did not reply. Nat started squirming around until they got into Space outside Earth's atmosphere. Nat was shocked that she could breathe.

"If you remember, I previously told you the ring has a life-support system, which means you can breathe anywhere. Now that we are up in

Space and don't have to be so concerned with gravity, let me teach you how to fly," said Infinity.

Infinity gently let go of Nat's hand, letting her float in Space, imagining her first steps walking.

"The easiest way to learn to fly in Space is the Superman position. I'm sure you have read a Superman comic or know who he is?" asked Infinity.

"Yes. By the way, how are we talking to each other?" Nat replied.

She stuck a slightly wobbly Superwoman pose.

"The ring has a com system inside of it. Okay now. Start thinking of moving without actually moving. Let a force push you around to where you want to go," instructed Infinity.

Nat started focusing and she started moving forward a bit. She started accelerating faster and faster until she soon was heading towards Mars. She started panicking, not knowing how to stop or slow down, until she looked to her left and saw seeing Infinity was there, flying on his back, as if he was lying down with his hands behind his head. They hurtled along and suddenly went straight through the planet and out the other side.

"Remember, we are Spectator mode. It means we are completely invisible and intangible, hence we can go through anything. But don't get too cocky with this mode. Other people can breach it. We don't want that incident to happen again!" said Infinity.

"Great and thank you for declining to mention how to Stop!" Said Nat.

"Pull your front hand back. And stop thinking about being pushed," replied Infinity, chuckling mischievously to himself." Infinity replied.

Nat started to slow down. Infinity grabbed Nat & helped her to create friction, to make them stop faster. He then spoke to both their rings: "Do a full body disinfection,"

“Why did you say that to the rings?” asked Nat.

“Because I want to open up a new portal to another world and I don’t want to spread the virus that is on us. Albeit, it should be dead now. But better to be ‘Safe than Sorry’,” said Infinity.

“Why would he have want to come there?” asked Nat.

“He most probably would have wanted to kill them, before they managed killed each other or to cause even more pain,” Infinity surmised.

Infinity proceeded to open up a new portal leading to another dimension, “Spectator mode off,” he instructed the rings. They went through the portal and it closed behind them.

XIII. Adapt

Infinity and Nat came out of the portal together and immediately started falling through tree branches and leaves. Luckily they each managed to grab onto a branch stopped themselves from falling down further. Swinging like the apes they once were, they found themselves on a jungle-like planet, somewhat smaller than the Earth but with two smaller moons.

"Where are we? This isn't earth, is it," Nat asked.

"Yes it is. It's just an alternate version of it. On this Earth, the moons didn't collide so it didn't add to their mass and it seems it's mostly covered by jungle. No saltwater. That's interesting," Infinity replied.

Suddenly Nat's branch broke and she continued falling. Infinity jumped down catching her before she hit the ground and floated her down gently.

"Try to be more careful, please," he said.

They started walking through the jungle, seeing all sorts of exotic plants, with animal sounds being heard in the distance.

After a few moments, Nat asked: "What are we looking for? Why would he be here?"

"This was one of the dimensions you have on your algorithm. In answer to what we're looking for, look here," replied Infinity.

Infinity pushed aside some leaves showing a steep cliff with a stunning waterfall. Nat looked at it, astonished how beautiful it was. Infinity threw his ring down the cliff.

"That's a pretty long drop. How do you think I should get it back?" Infinity said.

"Why would you even do that? What's the point of throwing your ring away, if you're just going to go get it back?" said Nat.

"While we wait for him to arrive, this is a good time to teach you something. A little something about adapting," Infinity replied.

Infinity started gathering materials, like vines, wood and stones.

"See, people think adapting means changing oneself to fit into the environment. This is completely wrong. Humans have been adapting their environment to themselves for eons now. They never changed themselves... well, except when they were fish or apes. They had a certain way of thinking and kept to it. What they changed was the environment, to fit their needs. When people needed homes, they built houses and densities and so on. They did not accept nature to be their home. When they wanted to make their work easier, they built tools. If they want to adapt to a certain terrain, they adapted their way of thinking to that terrain, making out what is the best thing to do. By the way, offensive mode, deactivate," Infinity said.

Nat's clothes and ring replied: "Offensive mode has been deactivated."

"We are still being hunted by those creatures back there. I recommend you start gathering materials and start making tools. We have 15 minutes or less," Infinity said.

"Why would you do that then," Nat said.

"So you won't be dependent on technology," said Infinity smugly.

Nat sighed and started looking for the materials. After several minutes of collecting materials, they started crafting weapons and tools. Infinity made a two-sided club with little spikes, whilst Nat made a spear with multiple tips, like a Trident, and some daggers. Suddenly out of the trees came out these monkey-esque creatures, with faces that resembled canines with sharp claws. There were about 12 of them. They started charging at Nat and Infinity. Infinity got into a defensive baseball pose and swung the club straight into the head of one of those creatures. Nat managed to stab the other one in the neck. The others in unison gave out a loud screech and they all started running towards them. Infinity hit another one with the other side of the club. The club broke at the middle and he threw it at the middle of them. Nat also started throwing some of the daggers she had made. The creatures took a step back and they retreated.

"Was it that hard?" Infinity said.

Nat gave Infinity a tired look, whilst hyperventilating. Infinity raised his hand towards the cliff and the ring flew back onto his hand.

"You could have done that.... All this time...?" panted Nat breathlessly.

She threw a rock towards Infinity's feet in frustration.

Infinity started laughing: "Okay. It looks like he's not coming here. Let's go to the next dimension."

Infinity opened up another portal and they both went through.

XIV. Good and Evil

A portal opened and Nat and Infinity came out, this time effortlessly, into a dimension where Germany won World War II and then betrayed Japan, making Earth a fully Nazi world. Their portal had opened up into a park that was gladly empty. It looked as if it was in 2019 most probably in where the UK used to be.

“Where are we?” Nat asked.

Infinity explained to Nat where they were.

“We should hide or something. We are going to stand out!” she exclaimed.

“No need. Just change your clothes into a uniform, with a Nazi emblem,” Infinity replied.

They both changed their clothes, with more than a modicum of embarrassment and disgust They started walking through the park and onto the surrounding streets.

“Why aren’t people protesting? Nat asked.

“Most probably, there are some people that are protesting and are most probably getting killed for it. Most people in this world agree with Nazism. They see it as a good thing. Very sickening, I know, but it all relates to morals and decisions of good and evil,” Infinity replied.

“What are the decisions of good and evil?” asked Nat.

“It mostly goes back to your culture. Like in one culture it’s okay to kill but in another not. Another decider of good and evil is history. Like in this world Germany won, so Nazism is considered a good thing. Everything relates to your age and the way you were raised. Those have a really high effect on your morals. See, it is important for dimension hoppers to define their morals and not be told what is right and wrong.

Some become like me and care about people. Some become like Key, a monster, and enjoy hurting people," Infinity replied.

As they were walking, a group of people started walking towards them. Infinity whispered to Nat: "Don't make eye contact and don't say anything."

They were able to pass by the people without any harm or drawing any suspicion.

They reached the City Hall, where they observed an execution of rebels against the regime taking place. Soldiers shot a volley at the rebels in unison, watching the wall of bodies collapse before them . In a rage, Infinity started singing *don't sing-data ft. Benny sings* reviving those who were shot and they started grabbing the guns and started to shooting at the soldiers.

"What happened about not helping people?" asked Nat.

"I never said 'don't help people', what I said was when there is no hope, don't waste your time on it. These people have hope and I sure as hell don't agree with Nazism," Infinity replied in a serious tone.

Nat smiled.

"Let's get these people to safety," said Infinity.

Infinity commanded his ring: "Locate the closest anti-Nazi rebellion camp and open a portal to there."

The ring did so.

Infinity then quickly got everyone to get go through the portal, Including Nat and himself. The portal closed instantly.

The Commander of the rebels came out with a few of her soldiers, guns pointing towards them and started talking to them: "Who are you?"

Thereupon the Commander recognized her own people and exclaimed: "How on Earth did you....?'

"How are we understanding them? Shouldn't they be talking German?" Nat asked Infinity.

"My dear we have translators, remember," Infinity replied to Nat.

Infinity turned his attention the Commander, replying to her: "Doesn't matter who we are. All that matters, is that were on your side."

The Commander smiled and told her people to stop aiming at them and gave a warm handshake to Infinity: "It's always good to have more friends these days!!"

"Your people are in bad condition. I recommend you take care of them. And if it's possible, can you give us a bed. We've been traveling and we would like to rest," said Infinity.

The Commander nodded and called for some medics who immediately went to treat her people. Nat and Infinity were escorted to a tent. After changing back into their regular attire, Nat was getting ready to sleep. "Why don't you ever sleep?" she asked Infinity.

Infinity raised his hand with the ring and replied: "This and the body I am using doesn't need sleep. But I could if I wanted."

"And do you want to sleep now?" Nat asked.

Infinity smiled and said: "Okay, if you wish."

Infinity laid down on the other bed and sweetly whispered: "Good night."

"Good night. So what... you're not going to sing me a lullaby?" Nat replied.

Infinity sent the lyrics of Mockingbird by Eminem to Nat via mental message and they both started laughing. After a few moments more, they fell asleep.

XV. Those in Need

It was around 6:30 when they were woken up by the Commander.

"Breakfast is being served at tent A7. We don't have a lot but it's a token of our gratitude. Afterward, we could use your help around the Camp. I would like to speak to you Mr……?" she said.

Infinity replied: "Infinity. Thank you for your hospitality. We would be glad to help you, Commander?

"Victoria" replied the Commander.

As the leader left, Nat thought of a croissant. She then put her hand in the satchel and took two out and handing one to Infinity. They started eating them. After a few moments, Nat realized that she could help them in a way, they need the most. She started thinking about canned food and bottled water and then held the satchel upside down letting it pour out. Infinity looked at Nat and smiled glad that she was a good person and had humanity.

After a while, the Commander Victoria came back to the tent. Before she entered she started saying: "Don't you want to come and eat. We shall be cleaning …."

As she pulled the tent flap up, seeing all the food and water said exclaimed: "Where did you get all of these?"

Infinity tilted his head towards Nat.

"Thank you!! It's a miracle! You're an angel!!" exclaimed the Commander, her stern face, becoming misty-eyed.

Infinity and Nat went outside and started walking around and helping out in the camp. After a while of working, Infinity came out and sat on a porch and looking at Nat from afar, he started singing very quietly *if only you knew – Ollie*. The Commander came and sat next to Infinity also looking at Nat.

"Do you have a crush on her?" she asked.

"Oh my, no! Never!" Infinity replied

"So what is all this singing about? It is obvious that the song is about love," she asked.

Infinity looked at Victoria, and she looked back at him quizzingly. He hesitantly replied: "Yes I love her. But all love is not from lust and romance."

After a few moments of silence, she asked again: "I figure you're not going to be staying with much longer but could you please stay just a bit longer? We need you in the war!"

"Sorry but no. I have my own war to fight but I can help you," Infinity replied.

Infinity dug deep into his pocket and handed Victoria a device with one singular button on it.

"I can give you three options. Number one I can adjust the device to kill all the Nazis but in doing so, it will also kill people that might change their minds in the future. Number two, kill all the Nazi leaders and generals and so on but they may be replaced. Number three, teleport all of you and those who don't want to live under this regime to another dimension but in doing so you will be leaving behind those that may change their mind in the future," explained Infinity.

Nat, overhearing them, came forward and added: "Secret option number four, show and convince everyone of the flaws of Nazism and make them against the Nazis out of their own free will and teleport all those who decide to remain a Nazi to another dimension, where rebels do not exist so both groups can live in peace."

Infinity smiled because he knew he had been successful in teaching her his lesson.

The Commander chose option four and Infinity to start singing *mad world -Gary Jules*and option four started playing out, portals opening and closing all over the world.

XVI. Getting Along

“You should go about organizing a new government,” said Infinity to the Commander.

Afterwards, Infinity and Nat went for a short walk. ”We have wasted so much time here!” Nat exclaimed.

“All for a good cause, though,” Infinity replied.

“I know, I know. It’s just that I’m worried,” Nat said.

Infinity then started singing * don’t worry be happy - Bobby McFerrin*.

After singing, Infinity commented “Ironically, the song never stopped anyone from worrying. Tell me what’s bothering you?”

Nat chuckled and said: “I am worried about my parents, friends, family, my dimension. I am worried that they will get destroyed or worse. What am I supposed to do, if you can find him? You told me that you have never won against them and I sure as hell can’t fight him. So we're screwed either way. I’m getting tired and scared.”

Infinity hugged Nat and said: “Even in my dying breath I’m going to be protecting you. I promise you that and as for Key, I have actually won against him before but he wasn’t so powerful at that time. I will not allow for your dimension to get destroyed. I promise you.”

Infinity stopped hugging her and started singing *count on me - Bruno Mars*to reassure Nat.

After walking for a good 6 minutes more, Infinity exclaimed: “It doesn’t look like he’s coming. We should go. The next place we're going to go is Hell itself, so we have to turn on spectator mode and float as well.”

“Wait, what? Hell? Did you just say Hell?” Nat replied.

"Yes," Infinity replied nonchalantly.

"So Heaven and Hell really exist?" Nat asked.

"Depends. I will explain later," Infinity replied.

"So was that Utopia place, Heaven?" Nat asked.

"Yet again it depends, but no that was just a perfect universe," Infinity replied.

"How can I float?" asked Nat.

"You remember how you flew. Just think that something is pulling you up, counter-acting to gravity," Infinity replied.

Nat started to float and Infinity opened up a portal leading to that dimension. Before entering it he activated his ring's spectator mode, as did Nat. They both went through the portal and the portal closed behind them.

XVII. Hell on Earth

The portal opened onto another dimension. It looked like Earth but a demented version of it. There was fire everywhere. A reddish sky. Demons flying through the sky and giant demons walking aimlessly around, crushing people underneath them. There were people screaming in agony whilst they were getting burned and were in pain and great suffering. Everyone was in his or her own personal hell. The place smelts of sulfur. It somewhat resembled Dante's Inferno. Nat and Infinity were floating there in the sky.

"Why does such places exist?" Nat asked

"To punish those who deserve it" Infinity replied.

"Why is the torture different for every single one of them?" Nat asked.

"It's because people are different, each having different weaknesses. Most of the people here deserve it. It depends if the Hell is natural or made. But it doesn't matter. They will still have flaws in them. By the way, this is what I meant by saying that a world full of Evil is painful," Infinity replied.

"What are the demons for then?" asked Nat.

"They are the wardens basically. Some are like an antivirus or a firewall. They stop anything from intruding from outside this dimension in order to alter it," Infinity replied.

Suddenly a demons crashed into Nat and got incinerated by Nat's Shield. This caught the intention of other demons.

Both Nat and Infinity sped away as they were chased by the demons.

"How are they seeing us? I thought we were invisible?" Nat asked.

"We are, I don't know what they saw. There most probably just going around inspecting there," Infinity replied.

Both Infinity and Nat flew to the right and stopped. The demons passed by them going straight ahead: "So they saw something or someone else. We have to chase them to see what is," Infinity said.

Infinity and Nat started flying towards the demons. The demons went around a corner and by the time that they turned the corner the demons had disappeared with only ashes on the floor beneath where they had flown. This caused immediate suspicion and alarm for Infinity.

"We should go. It does not look like he is here or if he was here, he's gone now. Anyways this place is not safe." Infinity then opened a portal into an empty dimension. Nat and Infinity jumped through the portal as the portal closed behind them. "Activate creator mode," Infinity commanded both rings.

XVIII. The World you Make

A portal opened into an empty dimension.

"Why is it empty? There are no stars, no planets, nothing!" Nat asked.

"It's because the Big Bang hasn't happened yet," Infinity replied.

"Why is it not going off then?" Nat asked.

"Because we are in creator mode. I'm going to teach you how to make your own universe but first I must explain you this. Remember when you asked me whether Hell and Heaven are real things. Well see, the Multi-verse made every single dimension and if such dimension is not altered , it will pave the way as well. Some, no actually all dimension hoppers, have their own universes where they have already paved the way. It's just like playing the game Minecraft or Sims but instead of one character or one family, one creates a complete universe. So when you ask is there such a thing as Heaven or Hell. Yes, it exists. Many of them. But does it exist naturally? It's the multi-verse so yes. What are they like, depends on the creator of that dimension but they're mostly harvested consciousness, in an endless loop. And is there a one true God? If you consider the pre-state of the Multi-verse and the Multiverse itself to be a God, then the Multiverse has never carved out its own religion and it is not conscious as far as I know. You see, those dimensions that have religion are either one, fake or two, completely wrong or three, the work of a cocky dimension hopper, craving for attention. Other dimension hoppers might come to other dimension hopper's dimensions and cause chaos, so they usually make defenses against them. Only allowing those they want to enter," Infinity replied.

"Like those demons?" Nat replied.

"Exactly, I'm getting carried away. The Big Bang will start when you allow it. Just think and it will happen. We are in creator mode right now, so we basically have power over how this dimension is formed. You can also put it in fast mode and give it an objective, so it can pave the universe so it will get to that conclusion or you can do it manually. I myself prefer the automatic way. By the way, don't make a defense against anyone entering because we want Key to enter here," Infinity replied.

"What I should think of? I have never made a world before so how am I supposed to make a universe?" Nat asked.

Infinity started singing *imagine - John Lennon* inspiring Nat. She then knew what she wanted to make. The Big Bang happened within an instant and the universe started forming before their eyes. Nat was in awe of what she had just witnessed but on the other hand Infinity looked quite bored as he leaned over to Nat saying: "We can skip this if you want to,"

"No I want to see this," Nat replied.

"Please put us in fast mode or if not we have to wait for millions of centuries to reach Earth's time to be created," Infinity replied.

Nat reluctantly put it in fast mode, witnessing the universe being made and formed, seeing stars being born then dying. Galaxies colliding. Black holes were created and evaporated. When it began to get to Earth's formation, it started slowing down. Both Nat and Infinity zoomed onto Earth's surface. They witnessed a hot ball of fire slowly getting cooled down. Two moons. The moons colliding, giving excess mass to Earth, making it bigger. An asteroid hitting Earth giving it water. The Planet slowly getting life. The dinosaurs were created, flourished and then became extinct. The Ice Ages coming and going, freezing and unfreezing the Earth, over and over again. Finally it reached these Homo sapiens, showing how they evolved into smart creatures, creating civilization gradually, along with making war. Reaching into an enlightenment era.

Cracking the code on electricity. Getting nuclear power. And then it stopped around the human Earth year of 2004.

Infinity said we should go look around and see how you made your world look like.

They both start flying towards the planet and landed there.

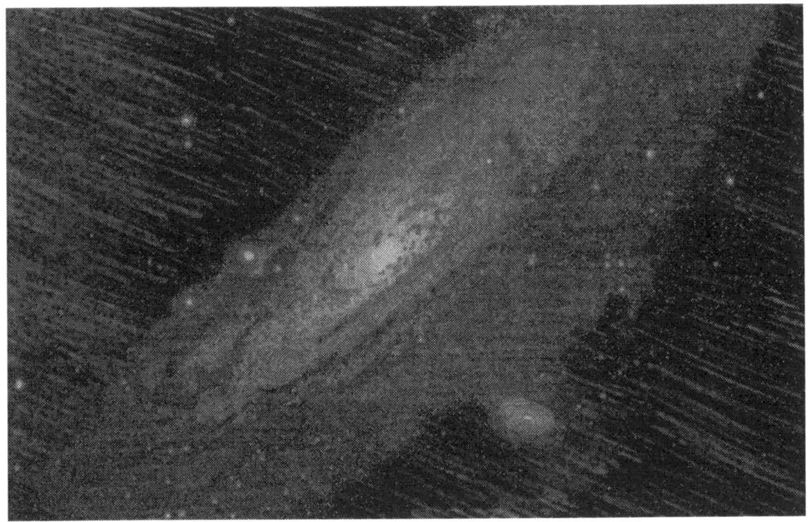

XIX. To a God

After landing, Nat and Infinity landed exited creator mode. They start walking around. What they saw was a world just like Nat's Earth, from her own dimension.

"He did well for your first world. I am impressed. Normally people making their first dimension, end up making a mistake that causes a huge problem. I didn't say anything to them or command them anything and left them to their own free will. It still has some flaws but that is not your fault anymore," Infinity said to Nat.

"Thank you, I guess. What do you mean flaws? Did you make a better world on your first try?" Nat said and smiled.

"No. I ended up leaving my dimension and what I meant by flaws is this," Infinity replied.

Infinity started singing *is this the world we created? – Queen*. Suddenly all the monitors started showing all the flaws of her world, caused by the people living there. After the song finished, he further explained:

"In this world, because they had free will, they had the ability to lie and they did so, either out of stupidity or intentionally. What those lies caused were wars. Various and conflicting religions were made and no one knew if any of them were correct, except for perhaps the scientists who are the most equipped people for figuring out this sort of stuff. They were the ones who caused the advancements of the world. You made a copy of your own dimension but just with different people. You copied its flaws as well. At least you didn't blow up your dimension like me! Sorry, I'm jabbering again. We should leave. Doesn't look like he's coming and it has been around 36 days now," Infinity replied.

Nat in an angry and shocked tone asked: "36 days!!!! Why didn't you tell me? You know I am worried and we have been here for 36 days!!! Why didn't I get hungry or anything?!?"

"I tried to tell you but you insisted on watching the universe form. And remember you were in creator mode, so you don't feel hunger or sleepy!" Infinity replied.

Nat feeling aggravated flew off leaving Infinity standing there.

XX. Generations

Nat was sitting on the edge of a cliff overlooking a lake. Infinity flew behind her and started floating down. He started singing*history has its eyes on you –Hamilton*. As he finished singing Nat's looked up at him and said: "If that was supposed to reassure me, it failed."

Infinity sat down next to Nat and replied: "Nope it's something that actually happened to me. I have failed so many and, to be honest, I'm scared to fail you. He has killed so very many people that I haved loved. It has been eons now that I have not dared to love anyone, so they don't get killed,"

"How's this supposed to make me feel better? I myself am scared silly. I don't know what to do when we get to him. Hell, I don't even know how to fight correctly and don't think I haven't noticed that you've been stalling to teach me your lessons. When I told you not to teach me them so we could find Key faster," Nat replied.

Suddenly a father and daughter came and saw Infinity and Nat there together.

"Oh, we will come back another time," said the father.

As they left, Infinity sighed and looked at Nat: "You used to come here with your dad, probably when you had anxiety?".

Nat nodded. Both Nat and Infinity stared out onto the lake. Seeing the girl and father playing on the beach.

"I am not stalling but yes I was teaching the lessons. You keep asking what must I do when we get to him and all that. Well, the things I'm teaching you are the stuff that you have to know so that you can survive in the Multi-verse. If I haven't said it before, I'll say it now. I will not allow Key to destroy your dimension even if my own life is at stake. Hasn't been that much of a bad time, has it?" Infinity said.

“No it hasn’t. I have had a great time, even though it has been a trifle tiring,” Nat replied.

“All the things I’ve taught you so far are the things that you need to know when you go up against him so that you’ll have a chance. I’ll also teach you how to fight if you’re willing? It will take no longer than a couple days. You already know martial arts but you do not know how to fight. I’ll teach you that,” Infinity said and laughed.

XXI. To Fight

The portal opened into the center arena of a coliseum in the middle of a jungle, with a waterfall not far away. There were a few benches on the sides of the arena.

"I come here to train. I usually use these photonic robots. It's kind of like S-Hot but in real time. And yes they do hurt but now I'm not going to turn them on until you first have to learn how to fight properly. Hit me," Infinity said.

"What?" Nat asked

"I said hit me. Give me your best shot!!" Infinity exclaimed.

Nat attempted to hit Infinity with an effete punch but Infinity just casually sidestepped the punch. After seeing this Nat threw another punch with more precision and vigor but Infinity avoided that as well with equal ease. Nat started punching in a frenzy, with Infinity avoiding every single one of them. Nat attempted to throw a few kicks but Infinity holding his hands behind his back again avoided every single one of them.

"You tried to attack me without thinking. You think you're just going to win, but you are not calculating what your opponent is going to do. When you see him leaning to the left, know he's going to strike from the right. When you see a hand being drawn back, know it is going to be used as a punch. Try to mix them. Make them expect one thing and do the other," cried Infinity.

Infinity then slid to the left causing Nat to trip in her frenzy. He then gave his hand to Nat helping her standup.

"Now look at my attack. Activate level XVIII bot. weapons deactivated," Infinity commanded.

The projector started projecting a photonic training robot. “Begin” it squawked, as its eyes glowed red. It started attacking Infinity who gracefully dodged its attack.

Infinity cried out whilst being attacked “Try to look for patterns. For its weaknesses. And then stick to that plan of attack, Use its attacks against itself, like so.”

Infinity then went into a frenzy of spin kicks, constantly and precisely hitting the robot in its head. Using both the front and back of his feet, he was spinning like a ballerina on cocaine. The robot grabbed Infinity’s foot in the middle of one of his kicks so Infinity jumped and pulled his leg, throwing himself towards the robot and he kicked it in its chin with his other foot, causing the robot's neck to snap. Infinity landed safely and bowed while the robot staggered and started fading away.

“Impressive,” Nat said.

“It’s your turn now. Activate level VI. You should be able to take care of this one easily. I want you to get to at least level X by the end of today,” Infinity coached.

Nat practiced and practiced until she perfected her moves, with Infinity patiently but persistently coaching her. Level to level until she made it to level XII.

“Great now start doing the same with weapons. Make your clothes give you a sword and a shield. Activate level VI. Activate weapons,” Infinity said.

Nat made her sword. It was white glowing sword with glowing light blue laser-edges. Infinity arose and made his own sword. “Multiple activate,” he exclaimed.

Several photonic robots appeared and started attacking both Nat and Infinity. They were surrounded, so they went back to back.

"When you have a partner. Try to use them as much as you can. They are your best weapon. Also, try to disarm your enemy. When they attack, attack from a side they do not expect," Infinity cried.

A robot came to strike Nat, but she deflected it with her shield, then kicked the robot in the knee, causing it to break. She then delivered the coup de grace by stabbing it in the head with her sword. It staggered and started fading away. Three more remained. Infinity blinded one with the edge of his sword, causing it to stop and stagger and fade away. Infinity bent now and Nat jumped on his back. He then push backed, launching her into the sky. With a backspin he proceeded to kick the robot in its head and then stabbed it in its chest while it was lay on the floor. Nat meanwhile sky-doved onto the other one, shattering it instantly with her sword.

"Okay that's enough for today," Infinity said.

"Am I now capable of taking on Key?" Nat asked.

"Rome wasn't built in a day," Infinity said and smiled.

They both went and sat down on the benches. Nat put her hand in her satchel, pulling out two energy drinks, handing one to Infinity. They both started drinking and taking a rest.

"You know all about me and my dimension but I didn't know anything about you. Tell me what is your story?" Nat said.

After a few moments of silence, Infinity replied: "......,"

XXII. The Good ol' Days

"I and your father were together for a really long time. Ever since I can remember, actually. We used to go out on these adventures....," Infinity said.

Infinity was cut off by Nat: "No I mean your own life. Not only your time with my dad."

"I don't want to say. I have friends but they were killed by Key. I currently live with my best friend. You have seen the base. I don't know what more to say," Infinity said.

"Tell me about your life before becoming a dimension hopper or why you even become one!" Nat pleaded.

"Well, I use to be a scientist/inventor. I like most dimension hoppers, attempted to prove the Multi-verse in our world, by making a portal and got out of there. I had my own company. Everything was good. One day there was this meeting. We finally made a working dimension portal and wanted to send a living smart creature through it. I heard some news that made me a good candidate. Not only was I capable of leaving but I knew the Multi-verse like the back of my hand. I got them to agree to send me convincing them in this meeting. They all asked me what to do and who we should send. At the time I did not have this ring, so I took out my phone and put on song *whatever it takes - imagine Dragon*and I walked up looked out the window. After the song was finished I told him the reason. They all talked together and agreed. Around 3 to 4 months later, my training started. I had this small little base that I was going to be traveling with. I made this AL, so if I was going to an isolated planet, I wouldn't be totally alone. I remember how scared I was that day I left. I hadn't even left and already I missed my family. Later on, I went to this world to start training and learning how to fight correctly. A lot of adventures happened there but like all good stories it ended but I still continued going on and on," Infinity replied.

Infinity started singing *yesterday – Beatles*thinking about the past.

"Those were the good old days but those days are dead and we are what is left," Infinity said.

XXIII. Paradoxes

"We should start leaving again. Let's mix up the list. Choose whatever dimension you want," Infinity said.

Infinity sends the list via mental message to Nat who started looking through the list until she said: "I choose this one,"

Infinity looked at it and was shocked to find which dimension she had chosen.,

"We can't go to that one!! It's a bloody paradoxical dimension!! How did that get in here? Infinity exclaimed.

Infinity looked at the list again and saw even more paradoxical dimensions. He wondered why they were on his list. He saw that when Key was destroying dimensions, he was also opening these portals up.

"Why can't we go to these dimensions?" Nat asked.

"I figure you have read or have taken a course in multiversal quantum mechanics. You do know about paradoxical events/choices, right?" Infinity questioned.

"Yes," Nat replied.

"Good, good. So paradoxical dimensions are dimensions, consisting of only those events/choices. If we were going there we would've been dissolved to our basic structures and those would be dissolved until we were only 0D. Our rings have a failsafe so we don't open those portals by mistake. He won't be there," Infinity said.

Nat got a bright idea. "Are any of those dimensions, from his past? He might be going there out of nostalgia," she said.

"Okay I'll filter them out for you," Infinity said and smiled.

Infinity thing gave Nat a shorter list. She then chose a dimension and opened a portal to there. She went through it and suddenly the portal closed behind her leaving Infinity behind.

XXIV. A World in his Image

Nat started freaking out. She was in this dimension where everything was pitch dark. She could only see 10 feet in front of herself because of thick heavy dark fog. There was barely any light. The sounds and screams of crying children could be heard. She activated her night vision on her lens. It helped her see much better, even though it was glitching out.

Nat started wandering, going towards the cries. While she was walking, she noticed this is to be a world with an advanced civilization but it was abandoned like it had undergone an apocalypse. From the moment she arrived into this world she felt sad and pain. She felt anxious and stressed out. It was quite cold. While Nat was walking the fog got thicker. She could only see up to 5 feet clearly now. Everything beyond that point was blurry. She continued walking, when suddenly someone grabbed her ankle. It was a man with a beard and with no eyes. He kept tugging at her, pleading: "Help me, please help me!"

Trying to pull himself closer to Nat he was suddenly pulled back and could be heard screaming: "Run!! Before it gets to you, RUN!!!"

Without thinking, Nat started running in the opposite direction that the man was pulled. Suddenly the remains of the poor man was thrown at Nat causing Nat to be thrown on the ground. The man was paralyzed and said in a weeping tone "It's coming, please end my suffering". His head was momentarily crushed underneath a huge hand. Before Nat stood a gray skinny human-like creature, with long arms and legs. Its feet were bird-like. Its hands had long overgrown nails. Its ribs were clearly visible. It face, if you could call it that, was blank and featureless, besides a mouth, which was dangling open, with sharp teeth, making the sound of a crying child. It gave out a screech and started crawling backwards. Nat couldn't move out of fear. It started, crawling towards Nat on all fours. Suddenly from the back, a lasso was thrown around its neck and jerked it back sharply. The monster was pulled back with it.

Infinity appeared from the side the monster was pulled from. He gave out his hand to help her up. Nat gave her hand and asked in a scared tone: "What was that?"

"That was a weeper. If you think those things are scary, then I am your nightmare," Infinity replied.

Infinity's face started melting, revealing blood, bone and tissue. His head started spinning upside down, his mouth opening wide revealing crooked, rotting teeth. His grip got harder. It was obvious that it was a creature impersonating him. Out of nowhere, the creature's head was blown off. The true Infinity started running and grabbed Nat's hand, pulling her to himself. Behind him were two weepers. Another weeper came out from the fog... Infinity seeing the monster, jumped in the other direction, avoiding all three of them. He dug deep into his coat, taking out a grenade and threw it. The grenade was a temporal time-loop grenade. It started playing the song *Harlem Shake – Baauer*. The monsters were trapped doing the last thing, over and over again, like a boomerang video. Both Nat and Infinity meanwhile continued running for all their lives' worth.

"What is the song for then? You're not the one singing it!" Nat asked.

"Lets me know when the effect is gone. It also draws enemies towards that location," Infinity replied.

Infinity tried to open up a portal but it kept on closing because of the dimension's characteristics. Nat and Infinity both went inside a building. They both took a deep breath but the air was so polluted, it was like a breathing hell in. Inside the building, there was fungus everywhere. Infinity then got scratched on his face. Over and over again. Nat started freaking out and asked: "What should I do? What should I do?"

Infinity reverted his clothes to the default mode and said: "Glow! Glow!"

Nat did so. She then saw these shadow creatures. They hissed at them and went away.

Infinity asked for Nat's hand. Nat willingly gave her hand and they both tried to open a portal together. This time, together, they managed to do it and not quickly enough they went through it.

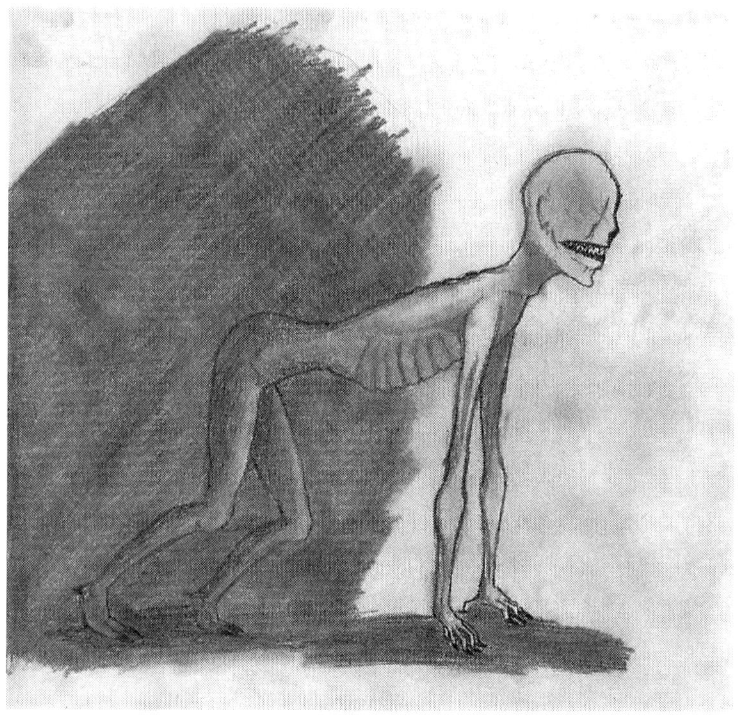

XXV. The Fallen Kingdom

Nat and Infinity hurtled down, falling on the ground, taking their breath.

"What was that place? What were those creatures?" Nat asked.

"That was Key's own dimension. Well, it used to be someone else's dimension. But he killed them, taking it away from them and corrupting it, making it into that place. Nobody visits there because number, one you have to be stupid and number two, if you enter, then you're alone. You're trapped there. Didn't you notice why the rings barely didn't work or technology in total?" Infinity replied.

"Yes, I did notice it," Nat replied.

"It's one of the effects of that world. We were lucky, we didn't see the really bad creatures. Those were just corrupted organisms," Infinity replied.

"I am never going back there again," Nat said.

"You and I both," Infinity replied.

They both closed their eyes for a brief moment, then Nat opened hers and looked around and stood up asking: Where are we?

Infinity, lying down, replied: "This is what's left of the Key Core. They are mostly dead,"

"They used to be more horrible people like him?" Nat asked.

"No, the Keys used to be good people. Their name used to bring hope. But unluckily for them, he was one too! The Keys themselves don't call him Key. They call him Evil Key or by his other name, Glitch. Now, if there are any other Keys left beside him, they have changed their names. Because now their name brings only fear and pain. This place used to beautiful. But this shit happened because of Evil Key," Infinity replied.

"I wish I could've seen it!" Nat said.

Infinity looked at Nat and then sat on his knees. He started singing *Viva la Vida – Coldplay*. The ruins started being reconstructed. Photonic projections showed other Keys. Then it started showing how everything went downhill. It started showing a revolution and it showed them trying to break through the head Key's main doors. Then it started fading away.

"We should leave to the next place. It doesn't look like he's here," Infinity said.

Infinity stood up and opened up a portal to the next place. They stepped through and the portal closed behind them.

XXVI. Shattered Heart

A portal opened. Nat and Infinity passed through it. They had arrived at an abandoned base. There were birds flying about, chirping cheerfully. The vegetation was lush, the air crisp and clean. It looks as if it was on Earth.

"What is so special about here? It's just some broken base," Nat asked.

"No, it's not some broken base. This is the place where Evil Key took the life of Hero key's love away. You see there. That is a grave. A memorial. She is buried there," Infinity replied.

"Who is Hero Key?" Nat asked.

"Hero Key is the only person that has defeated Evil Key, but after that, he went into hiding. No one has ever heard of him since. Hero Key was the best Key out there. Whatever dimension he visited, he would make sure they had a happy ending. He was willing to give his life to anyone who deserved it. Because of the way he was and opposed Evil Key's ideology, Evil Key was hell-bent on breaking Hero Key. Now that Hero Key has gone into hiding, Evil Key is now free to do whatever he pleases," Infinity replied.

Infinity picked a flower and placed it on the gravestone.

"Legend has it she was killed right on that spot. In every story, it ends with her death. Like Hero Key, she was legendary as well. Always thinking about others before herself," Infinity said.

Infinity chuckled but it was obvious he was in pain and continued: "Evil Key sure does have a thing for killing loved ones."

Infinity stood there in silence. Nat started wandering off looking at the empty ruins. She could see Key symbols everywhere. Infinity then called out to Nat. He started singing *clocks – Coldplay*and a holographic story of Hero Key's wife began playing in reverse. It showed how she died to the point she became a dimension hopper.

“We should leave. He won’t be coming here. He apparently wants this place to remain as it is, as a reminder to Hero Key of his loss. Plus he may not be able to open portals to here,” Infinity said.

Infinity opened up another portal, through which both Nat and Infinity passed through. The sounds of birds chirping could still be heard.

XXVII. Broken Trust

The portal opened onto a dead, apocalyptic desert planet. It looked like it was once Earth with a huge crater in the middle.

"Where are we? I am guessing this is his work!" Nat asked.

"You guessed correctly. This is where he was made into the villain that he is," Infinity replied.

Nat looked at Infinity, with arched eyebrows and asked: "Made?"

Infinity looked back at Nat and replied: "Yes, "Made." He chose to be Evil Key here. I know it's hard to understand but monsters are not born, they are made. They become one. Usually if they are exposed through time to constant self-doubts, fear, anger, neglect and so on. Monsters are people that need help but don't know how to get it, so they cause pain. Some monsters go so far that there is no point of return anymore."

Suddenly both of them noticed an old man on the other side of the crater. The man noticed them as well. The man stared at Infinity and Infinity stared back at him. They both nodded at one another. The old man opened up a portal and left.

"Do you know him?" Nat asked.

"Know him and respect him," Infinity replied.

"Would you care to explain who he is to me," Nat said.

"That I am afraid is a story for another day. As I was saying, you have the Seven Deadly Sins that everybody despises. Well, these are all cries for help. Pride is for someone who feels that they are not good enough; Envy is for someone who wants to be like someone but they don't know how to become as such; Wrath is for someone in the throngs of pain and fear who doesn't know what to do except panic with rage; Gluttony is for someone who is emotionally in pain and alone and is trying to fill this void with food; Lust is for someone who craves love and company; Sloth is caused by undue concern and fear of failure; Greed is caused by neglect and feeling like you have nothing that matters to fill the void that the neglect causes," Infinity mused.

There was another moment of silence. Nat and Infinity gazed absently into the crater before Nat again broke the silence: "Anyway, what is the story about this place?"

"A long time ago, Hero Key and Evil Key used to be the best of friends. They used to be called by their other names back then, so no confusion existed at that time. They both used to hop all around the multi-verse helping people. Both so much the same yet at the same time so different. Everything is predestined in the Multi-verse. Something that was unique about these two is they both knew how things were going to turn out. It's as if they know the true future. So that's why they're really good at combat, taking risks, etc. because they know about the future. They know their own future. Anyhow, one-day Evil Key ultimately gives into who he is destined to become. He committed his first genocide here. The man they used to be was no more and Hero Key and Evil Key were born," Infinity explained.

"We should start looking for him at other places. He is not coming here," said Infinity as he opened up another portal. "The next place we are going, is going to be magical. Literally,"

"What do you mean by that?" Nat asked.

"You will see," Infinity replied.

They both went into the portal and it closed magically behind them.

XXVIII. Magic

The portal opened onto an enormous market. The weather was both quite hot yet chilly at the same time. Both moist and dry. There were creatures there from all sorts of dimensions. Creatures that one knew to only be found in fairytales: Ogres, Fairies, Honest politicians; Aliens of all sorts and sripes; Felines, octopods, reptilians, mammals, artificial life. You name it. They were all there. It was a quite busy place. The chattering of people could also be heard above the din.

"Welcome to the Magic Market!" Infinity said.

"Magic market? Don't be ridiculous, magic doesn't exist! But do explain to me why my senses are both dry and wet, hot and cold at the same time?" Nat asked.

"It is so they can save space here. They reuse the same space but in another dimension. By dimension I mean 3D, 4D, etc., so right now the reason you feel two different states of temperature and moisture is because of the other spaces. And yes that is magic," Infinity replied.

"Why are you insisting its magic? We both know magic cannot exist," Nat asked.

"Well, magic is a science we have not understood yet. If you showed your phone to someone from the Middle Ages they would think that it was magic. Hell, chemistry was considered witchcraft for a long time in those times. But we learned its secrets and mastered it and what, which seemed to be magic, turned out to be science. Go ahead. Let's take a walk. Whatever you want, I will explain it to you," Infinity said.

They started walking further into the market. They could hear people advertising for themselves and hawking their products: "Feel young and beautiful again, with my product. Dr. Sharon Lannon's LeBlanc cream";" Come on right up and get ya invisible cloaks! Sneak around anywhere you wish, no one will know!";" Repeat my spells and be granted those magical powers"; "Are you low on Magic, get your Magical refill here!";" See the unseen with my magic potion. You'll be coming back for more"...

"Okay Mr. Know-it-all, explain those advertisements. What are they?" Nat asked mischievously.

Infinity looked at Nat with a smirk and said: "The first one is a cream that helps the regeneration of their DNA and thereby replenishes and rejuvenates the cells, making them younger and keeping you from aging as rapidly. The second one bends light, so that you won't be seen. Remember spectator mode? It's the same thing. The third one is a voice-activated machines. Depends on the spell what the machine will do. Some will open portals, some will cause forces pushing stuff around, some will heat stuff up It all depends on the spell. The fourth one IS actually magic, I will explain that later. The last one is just simply liquid LSD. Don't ever use it, it can ruin your life."

"Yet again with the magic mumbo-jumbo. Why are you insisting that it exists?" Nat said.

"You see Magic in this meaning is actually X̲D energy. As you know X̲D is basically what composes the Multi-verse. So in a way, it can do anything you want it to. This X̲D energy, a.k.a. Magic Energy, is the force that can break or disobey the rules of reality. X̲D creatures are known to use this frequently. Just look at cartoons. It is basically that. Actually some of those spells also use this. But you can still make sense out of it. It's just another science we do not understand. Actually you understand this is just ughhh," Infinity replied.

"I guess you can accept that in a way but you're redefining the word into something with the same meaning. You're right it is ughhh," Nat said.

Nat and Infinity continued strolling through the market. They saw a number of famous faces pass by. Nat asked: "So what else do they sell in this market?"

"Anything actually. You think of it. It's there. Magical or non-magical. Famous or ordinary. Powerful or weak. You'll find it," Infinity replied.

After a few more minutes of strolling Infinity said: "We should start leaving. There still more places to see and search. Do you want to choose where to go next? Just don't close the portal this time until I have entered as well,"

Nat chose a dimension and opened the portal to it. Suddenly a giant hand came and grabbed Nat pulling her in the portal causing her to lose focus and close the portal before Infinity entered it. The giant hand startled everyone in that area of the market. Infinity just face-palmed and shook his head in despair.

XXIX. The World of Toons

Nat woke up with a horrid headache. She was lying on her right side. "Oww," she said, as she rubbed her head. She opened her eyes seeing that she was in a very cartoonish world, which at the same time was very real. She looked to her left and she got startled by seeing a person lying awkwardly next to her in a side pose. The person was a male feline, in a blazer and tie, monocle, white gloves and a black top hat. Very cartoonish looking. He was quite u_g_l_y_ handsome.

The cat coughed and said in drawl southern accent: "Howdy, Ma'am!"

He started coughing louder and more strongly and ended it with a little sizzle. He started talking in his cartoonish yet somewhat sophisticated accent, saying: "Pardon me darling, I didn't mean to startle you."

He stood up and helped Nat standup. He then bowed down gracefully and said: "My name is...,"

His hat started to open, revealing a smaller feline with a top hat just like his and that hat opened up revealing a smaller feline with a top hat just like his and that hat opening up revealing a card that was impossible to fit in its hat, saying "Mr. Reliops Dong". "But do feel free to call me Reli," he said.

Mr. Reliops Dong then looked over his left shoulder straight at the audience, saying to the readers/viewers "If you dare call me unoriginal because there are so much feline Cartoon characters but I will personally come and claw your eyes out. Anyway the rabbit and mouse were taken!!" and he feigned a few small scratches in the air. He then looked back at Nat and then back at the audience and continued saying "I heard that Timothy, I am not a Cat in a Hat rip-off!!" He glanced back at Nat and said, "Pardon my manners, Ma'am".

"Okay… I'm just going to ignore what you just did. My name is…" Nat meekly replied.

Nat got immediately interrupted by Reli, who said: "Oh let me guess! You are Nathaniel. I am Conner, the android sent by Cyber Life. No? Give me a sec!!"

He then went through his pockets, pulling out a well-worn leather book. He opened it and started ruffling through the pages. "Ah yes Nat, I had inexcusably mixed you up with another franchise," he apologized. He started going through the pages again and asked "Have you gotten to the point where it is revealed that Infinity used to be a Key? No?" He then went through the pages and said, "Oh, my bad! That is still in five chapters forward. Never mind, just ignore it." He continued to go through the pages and then suddenly closed the book and threw it away. He started sucking his fingers, saying "This book is quite juicy, the twists gives me the shivers!" He looked back at the audience once more, shaking a now oversized finger, saying "No peeking now!!".

Nat just started at him, confused at what he was doing, and quite flabbergasted.

"No need for confusion, just talking to our dear Audience! We have to entertain them, you know. I believe Infinity explained that to you back in Chapter Six',"

"Excuse me, Mr. Reliops, would you, per chance, know why can't I remember anything since the Magic Market. The last thing I remember is the portal opening," Nat replied hesitatingly, surprised at her choice of vocabulary.

"Yes the plot point!! We can't have a chapter without one, you know!" Reli replied.

Nat examined the world she was in and noticed that she was in a cartoonish-looking dimension. She deduced that Reli is an XD creature.

"Finally!! Even the author was wondering why you hadn't figured it out yet. If infinity was here, he would go off singing and showing you how quirky this world is but since he is not here, I will gallantly fulfill his role," Reli said.

Reli changed his clothes so he could looked like Infinity and started singing *can you imagine – the imperials*. While singing he grew in size and start showing off his powers.

After the song ended, he shrunk back to his normal size and said: "Okay, run along dear. You can go onto the next chapter now. This section is done."

 p-p

XXX. It's Just a Joke

A portal opened and Infinity came out. "Finally!! You know how long it has been that I have been trying to get into this damn dimension but couldn't because of this feline ass," Infinity said.

Reli scuffed and crossed his arms and said with indignation: "Why I never. I appreciate and adore you all this time and this is how you repay me. I'm frankly quite offended. And by your language and tone of address."

"Do I know you?" Infinity replied.

"Ouch that's got to hurt," Nat said.

Reli got very angry and began to swing back-and-forth, while he held his hands behind his back: "I am Mr. Reliops and I really did adore you for those few seconds that I read your book," he shouted.

"Please tell me you didn't reveal a spoiler," Infinity said.

"As a matter of fact I did reveal a spoiler. And what are you going to do about it?," Reli replied with a relish.

Reli then realizing what he had just said poofed away.

"Okay let's go. We don't want to waste any more time in this infernal place, do we?" Infinity said. Infinity felt a cold revolver behind his head.

You have me mixed up with another character from DC, didn't you?" Reli snarled, fingering the trigger. And then he squeezed the trigger, shooting Infinity straight through the head. Infinity momentarily just stood there gazing deep into Nat's eyes, and then fell down into a now substantive pool of his own blood at his feet. Infinity's ring came off his hand, picked up the body and teleported it away. Reli tried to grab the ring but got an electric shock by touching it.

Nat was screaming hysterically, crying over Infinity's death. Reli stood up and took out a carrot and started chewing on it, saying: "Wow wasn't he such a maroon!"

After a few seconds, Reli threw away his carrot and said: "I believe if Infinity was here, he would say a run!"

XXXI. Don't Judge a Book by its Cover

Without thinking, Nat started running, but it was futile. Reli was just toying with her. He would grow to a huge size, watch her run in a small field and then he would stretch the land's dimensions, to entertain himself. He even put a treadmill underneath her feet without her noticing and just changed the scenery as she ran. She became no more than a hamster.

Reli then shrunk back to his normal size and asked Nat: "Are you not tired yet?"

Nat still emotionally broken by the death of her friend tried to punch him but it had no effect of consequence. It merely made him wobble like Jell-O.

"As if the author would allow his main character to die off half way through the book! Just wait and he will be revived or something. But why don't YOU ever do anything by yourself?" Reli asked

A few seconds later a portal opened and Infinity stormed out, kicking hard Reli in the face. Infinity was the same but with brown hair and with a somewhat different facial structure. "Oww! That really hurts" Reli whined. He then started laughing and taunted Infinity, "As if you can hurt me! I am beyond you, fool". Infinity opened up the portal and teleported away. That was as much as a shock to Nat as what he had just done. Reli's attention went back to Nat just as a portal opened behind him, with Infinity coming out again and kicking him in the head once more, this time causing Reli to fall down.

"Perhaps but your own energy can hurt you," Infinity shouted.

Reli's eyes widened fully, knowing what was going to happen and tried to pounce on Infinity before he used it against him but he was too late.

Infinity cast a spell "Ezeerf!"Reli froze in place immediately. Infinity said to himself: "Thank you, old friend,"

Nat ran towards Infinity, hugging him. She then slapped him, saying: "Don't ever do that to me again. You have to explain to me how you survived!"

"Ow, fine I'll explain it, even though I have already explained it. Let's just get out of here first. I don't like it here," Infinity said.

Infinity opened a portal and they both stepped through it. The portal closed behind them. Leaving Reli frozen there.

XXXII. The Sound of Music

The portal opened and they came out into an outwardly rather ordinary-looking world. They were standing in a pasture high amongst a range of magnificent green mountains. It felt as if they were on the fringes of a forest because there were so many trees. Animals were making noises in rhythm and harmony. "How could you have died, do you know how much it hurt mind? How much I have cried, how my emotions stewed in my mind? I was terrified. I feel that you have lied," sang Nat.

Nat realized she rhymed the complete sentence without even trying.

"No I didn't lie! Yes I did die. So please don't cry, there is no reason for you to frown, because there is nothing to keep me down. So just calm down. I will always rebound. I have extra bodies lying around, in case I get shot, burned or drowned. My consciousness is transmitted, something painfully admitted, but I'm the one who benefited. My ring will fly away, my old body will decay, but I'm still here today. Nothing is going to take me away. So everything's okay," Infinity rhymed.

"Why do we rhyme when we talk? It is quite a shock, every single time, there is always a rhyme, and it is always chimes, just like the perfect crime," Nat asked.

"Oh it's just the land, for some, it might be bland. Those who matter will understand, and those who don't, it's just there stand, it makes them feel grand. It is just an extension of this dimension. Welcome to the land of the song, bong a ding dong. You got a new song, however long. Welcome to the land of the song," Infinity replied.

"What a horrible day, I felt the skies turn grey, but it seems it was all child's play. I even couldn't say goodneigh," Nat said.

Infinity in reply sang *do you realize - The Flaming lips* comforting her.

"Something that Reli said, has been trapped in my head. It could have been the reason you were dead. Is it true I don't do anything? Does it not make me worthy of this ring? Lord, I don't even know how to sing! Am I even enough, something that can't be replaced with stuff? Must I be more tough? Or must I be more rough?" Nat asked tearfully.

Infinity replied by singing *fucking perfect – p!nk*and hugged Nat, reassuring her once more.

"What if it happens again? How am I supposed to accept the pain? Am I supposed to take it with the grain? This is way too much for my brain," Nat replied.

Infinity replied again by singing her *under control - Calvin Harris & Alesso ft. Hurts* and finally managed to calm her down. Infinity stopped hugging her.

"Can we please go, this place is like a show, that makes me go oh no! I want to blow and glow with rage and sage from this combo, I can't do this in auto, you know I'm not a pro, so let's get up and go," she said.

Infinity smiled and opened another portal, and they both left. Afar in the distance a silhouette could be seen.

XXXIII. The Desert

The portal onto a very hot and dry desert-like planet. There were giant clay mountains and no water was anywhere in sight.

“Kind of reminds me of Dune,” said Infinity.

“What is Dune?” asked Nat.

“How could you not know? It is a really good book, you should read it one day,” said Infinity.

“We’re lucky, that there are no giant worms here,” said Infinity after a few minutes.

Infinity and Nat started walking towards a ravine between two jagged clay mountains. It was a long and hard walk. It was extremely hot.

“We should take a break,” said Nat.

Nat took out two bottles of water from the satchel and gave one to Infinity. She also took out an energy bar and start eating it. They both found a shady place under a cliff and sat down there.

“I’m going to take a nap, please wake me up in 10 minutes or so,” said Nat.

Infinity also decided to take a nap. It has been a long journey and he too was exhausted. They lent against the side of the mountain. Nat resting her head on Infinity’s, as one, they both drifted off into a deep slumber.

It had been only eight minutes when Infinity woke up by the sound of a loud noise. Infinity opened his eyes to see Reli’s top hat in front of him with a note on it saying “Miss me?” Infinity was petrified by this.

He asked his ring “What is the name of this planet?” The ring replied, “It is Dune”. A shiver went down his spine.

Infinity hurriedly woke up Nat. “We're leaving now!” he said.

"It hasn't even been ten minutes yet," Nat said in a tired tone.

Infinity continued to insist on leaving. Suddenly from the ravine, a distorted, somewhat glitchy voice called out: "So soon? You haven't even tried to amuse me or to catch my attention. You are losing your touch, Hero!"

Infinity instantly opened up a portal underneath Nat sending her back to his base. Not having enough time to react she was teleported away instantly.

Nat found herself at the entrance of Infinity's base.

From the speaker system Infinity's friend asked in a British accent "Where's that scalawag? Did he find him?"

Nat nodded. "I have to go back to him he needs my help!" she exclaimed.

"No can do, my Lady. I have temporarily deactivated the teleportation device in your ring. I am under strict orders from Infinity not to allow you to leave if he sends you here, the only exception being unless the base is under attack," Infinity's friend firmly but politely replied.

Infinity started singing *somebody's watching me –Rockwell* everything around him living with at least basic intelligence started to show themselves to him. He could see worms underneath the ground but were they were scared to come up. He saw a man lurking in the ravine. When the song stopped, the man started coming out of the ravine.

The man from the ravine was wearing a full body, fully black, reversed pico-photonic suit, with a full head helmet and a digital mask. On the mask, there were two "Xs" above the eyes and a digital smile. Nothing else could be seen on the face. He started walking into plain sight. He had a smoky red key logo on his chest. It was Evil Key.

XXXIV. The Dimension Destroyer

"You are afraid Key!" Evil Key said.

Infinity was quiet, just staring at him, with anger rising up within.

"Do tell me, do you miss me? Because I sure did miss you!" Evil Key remarked.

Infinity, still quiet, but now simmering with more rage was hurriedly planning an attack, looking for any way he could gain the advantage.

"You sure are quieter, since last time I saw you! Do you recall when that was?" Evil Key asked.

Infinity's ring started glowing red, and his eyes started flickering red.

"Oh wait, I remember now when that was! It was when I killed the love of your life! In a fit of rage, you killed me there! I was laughing for days! The pitiful look that was on your face!" Evil Key taunted.

Infinity's eyes glowed completely red and he suddenly charged towards Evil Key at great speed, letting loose a blood-curling battle-cry. Infinity hit him hard and dragged him down with himself. But Evil Key just continued laughing. He back slapped Infinity, throwing him aside, then he himself flew down.

"Did you actually think that would stop me? You once hit me much harder, long ago" teased Evil Key.

Infinity tried to hit him again but every attack no matter how tactical, was deflected. The same was true for Evil Key but at least he got a few hits through.

"I see you got a new partner now, huh?" said Evil Key.

"She is not my partner." Infinity replied.

"Say you don't care about... what's her name?... Nat!" said Evil Key.

“I don’t care about her,” shouted back Infinity.

“Who are you lying to? I was watching you ever, since the first world she visited looking for me!” said Evil Key.

Infinity’s eyes widened, when he realized that she’d been followed for so long.

“Oh yeah, and every single world she helped, I made sure they saw their nightmares,” said Evil Key.

Infinity began to boil with rage and started attacking faster and more precisely, finally managing to get a few hits in.

“Oh yes and I made sure every single one of them was in pain. The people from utopia, well let’s just say that dimension isn’t as perfect anymore. That jungle world, I burnt it to a crisp. You didn’t even have the guts to kill an animal over there!! And that world which you made Nazi-free, let’s just say I reinstated them to that place. Nat’s first dimension, I destroyed it!! Those worlds that relate to our history, I let them be, knowing that they’ll bring you more pain if they existed. The market, I set on fire and watched every single one of them run about in panic and chaos. That cartoonish dimension in which you left that poor guy all alone, with no protection, and no way for him to defend himself. He was a very easy kill. And that land of the song, I made sure to silence their racket!”

Infinity got punched in the face so hard that he fell on the ground.

“So what was your plan exactly? To kill me? We both know, I would just come back! Do tell,” asked Evil Key.

Infinity did not reply, so Evil Key kicked him. Then he bent down next to Infinity, standing on his left hand. Infinity tried to stab Evil Key but he took Infinity’s hand with the knife and pushed it towards Infinity’s other arm.

“Every single dimension you visit, I will make sure to bring it pain. You have also now given me another target to hunt down. Let’s see if you can save her or fail like the last time. Cheerio!" cried Evil Key and then he snapped Infinity's neck.

Infinity's ring flew off from his hand, grabbing all of his belongings, opened a portal and disappeared, leaving Evil Key there, alone with Infinity's naked corpse. Evil key started humming a very gleeful song*heart and soul –Hoagy Carmichael and Frank Loesser*.

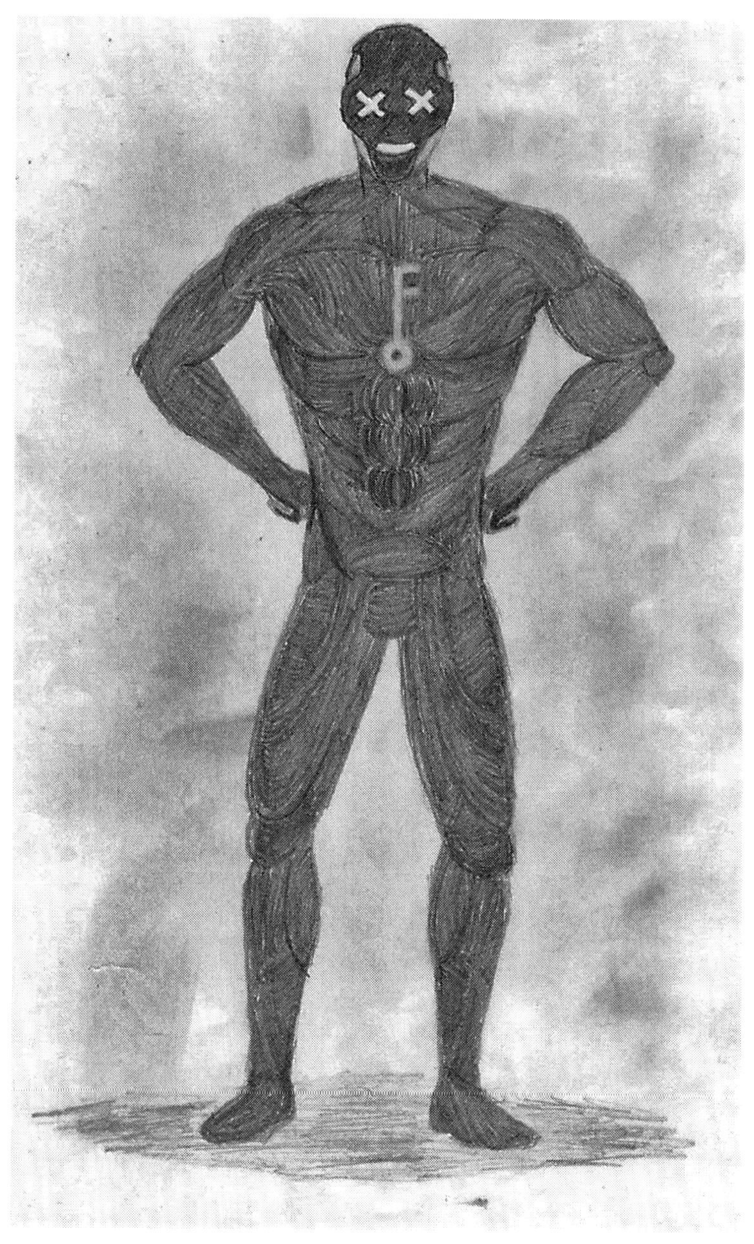

XXXV. The Poked Bear

The room was filled with numerous vats each containing a clone body which lay motionless under an aura of dim blue light. One of the clones with a mat of black hair, blue eyes and somewhat paler than the rest, woke up. Infinity's consciousness was transferred inside of the body. He started banging on the glass until the vat opened. Water spilled out everywhere but was instantly cleaned up by a "mop-up" robot. The body fell to the ground and slowly stood up. He staggered to a door which opened into walk-through closet. He took a wearable towel and wore it. He then went out through the closet and entered another hallway.

At the end of the hallway he unlocked a door and entered the living room. Nat was sitting on the couch looking rather dismal. Infinity raised his right hand up to a ninety degree angle from the ground. A portal instantly opened in the entryway and Infinity's ring flew at great speed through the hallway into the living room and onto Infinity's hand, before closing again. Infinity's clothes were back on and he took off the towel and dropped it to the floor, as a clean-up robot sped to pick it up for further laundry processing. Infinity sat on the couch next to Nat, with a great sigh.

Nat was shocked to see Infinity sitting there next to her and hugged him and then slapped him.

"Ow," said Infinity. Infinity bent over and was terrified. Actually all he could think was what Evil Key had said.

In the intercom system, Infinity's friend said: "Welcome back, I take it that your fight didn't go well, I warned you about this."

Infinity didn't reply, he was too frightened and occupied.

After a few moments Infinity said: He's going to hunt you down now. It's my fault. I'm sorry.

"Why did you teleport me away? I could've help….," asked Nat.

She was cut off by Infinity who curtly replied in frustration:" Because if I didn't, you would have been dead by now, and you would have no consciousness backup, and it is your original body,!". He then broke into song *whataya want from me – p!nk*.

Infinity sighed and restarted singing *human – Rag'n'Bone*. At the end a single tear came down his face. Nat tried to comfort him by hugging him tightly. After about three minutes, Infinity pulled himself together.

"I did everything in my power and he just pushed me aside like I was nothing! It's impossible for me to take him alone. I need the help of my friends," Infinity said with determination.

He stood up and started singing *help – Beatles*.

XXXVI. The Keys

“Please! I know you are frustrated and all that but I want to know who I am with! Why didn’t you tell me you were Hero Key! Please tell me about the Keys,” Nat pleaded.

Infinity sighed. “Because I didn’t want you to think any less of me. The name Key has been related to so many bad things. Basically it has become an insult.”

Infinity cleared his throat and continued softly: “My story is... Once I first went through a dimension portal, my friend and I went to this place, with heroes. Real champions. I learned to fight there. An accident happened there, which caused me to develop multiple personalities. I still was the dominant one but I wasn’t in pain, Later on, my time came and I had to leave. I tried to repay them as best as I could. I gave them happy endings, so they could live their lives peacefully.

I went exploring for a while. I made really close friends all around. Until one day, I met him. At that time he was someone depressed and in need of a friend. When nobody wanted to be his friend I decided to be. He didn’t have this ideology back then. We grew to become really close friends. We went on adventures together. Saved people. One day he got tired of all this. Because some of the people we tried to save, didn’t want to be saved, or when we saved them, someone else would come up and undo all of our work. He started saying we should put a stop to this, and just exterminate them. He made an example. I obviously stood against him. He wanted to commit the genocide of millions of dimension hoppers. The moment he did the genocide, he became Evil Key. I no longer loved him from that point on. Because I was no match for him, he turned into this monster.

I disowned him as a friend and cut my ties with him. He was though the only person who truly understood me and yet he didn’t understand me. He still didn’t except he would become Evil Key. He still believes he is doing the right thing, in his own warped manner of thinking. I don’t know what kind of journey he was on but he turned out more twisted than everyone. He didn't want to do anything good anymore. He just wanted to share the pain that he felt. Then, the spectator incident happened.

At the same time, I met the love of my life. I was still recovering from the breakup of another affair but as soon as I met her, the pain went away. I was also lucky to have those little voices in my head that gave me much emotional support. We all went on these adventures together. Everything was just dandy. Then the Key war happened. Everyone part of that empire died; basically Evil Key, my love and I. We became the only remaining Keys. Evil Key then vowed to hunt her down and did so when we least expected it.

Anyway, one thing led to another; for a time, we felt safe. We decided to give the other personalities their own bodies. Since then they have developed their own consciousness. I had dealt with the pain. I didn't want them to be part of me anymore. I wanted to give them their own choices. Evil Key ended up hunting them down. A few are alive now, one of them is named Joy, and she is the closest one to me. After my love died, I asked everybody to leave me. So they won't be in danger.

Though now I need their help again. Oh yeah, remember that old man. He is me, well a version of me but that is a story for another time. All this was the abbreviated version of my story. Let's go find them. I believe you have already semi-met my friend. Let me introduce you formally. ".

Nat asked: "Who are you? Who is Key? Can you just whisper it in my car?"

Infinity laughed and said a poem in Farsi:

کی، کیست وقتی که کی کیست   ان یکیست که می داند کی ، کیست
چه بسا کسی نیست   که بداند چی ، چیست
کسیست که انگیزش بماند اسکی باز در پیست   که چیزی باعث نشود ، که او کند ایست
که بداند عقل با ان نیست   که فقط بر برگه گیرد نمره ی بیست
ان یکی که می داند کی ، کیست   ان است که بداند خودش ، کیست
حال که رسدیم به اخر و نتیجه ی این لیست   بدان زندگی تخمیست

Nat chuckled. Then they both walked towards the rooms to meet Infinity’s friend.

XXXVII. The Smartest Being

Nat and Infinity walked into the hall of the rooms. They went into the last room on the right. They entered it but nobody was in there that could be seen. It was just a bank of monitors with a single seat in the middle.

"Wait! I thought this was the monitoring room," exclaimed Nat.

"It may half appear so but actually it is his room. Nat, I would like to introduce you to Centimuss" replied Infinity.

"Greetings," said Centimuss through the speaker system.

"Where is he?" Nat asked.

A digital face appeared on one of the monitors.

"I am right here. Exactly in front of you. You should get your eyes checked!" replied Centimuss in an English accent.

"He is an AL a.k.a. artificial life, basically an AI with AE, with a freethinking conscience. If you don't know what AI or AE stands for, AI is artificial intelligence, AE is artificial emotions. He is also a hive mind. I'm sure he would like to explain that," explained Infinity.

"Well it's not actually a hive mind, more like 'gathered consciousness". A hive mind would have more than one computing system. What I am is, well, you see sometimes, dimension hoppers experience other people's lives or see how it feels like if they were born someplace else and were then just raised and well, die there. Some of them edit the memories they have from those times, so they can feel like they're watching a movie," said Centimus enthusiastically.

"...With a soppy story line," he murmured to himself.

"Some of them choose to entirely not remember it, basically wasting their time. Some, like myself, decide to keep those memories through our main consciousness. The original one, has all function but is also influenced by the other memories. The consciousness is basically the same… we just differ in the decisions,"

"Oh okay then. Noted!!" Nat interjected, admittedly with some confusion.

"Centimuss, I need your help, I want to put the core back together," Infinity said with seriousness.

"I would love to but I'm currently processing, multiple lifetimes, my Emperor is about to finally reach the Glory Land," replied Centimuss.

"Goddammit, for the millionth time, stop invading Poland!" Infinity replied in a frustrated tone.

Nat burst out in laughter, a tear running down her face and said: "Why are you invading Poland?"

"A reason? There is no reason to invade Poland, it is just something that must be done, like setting fire to the lawn of the neighbor you do not like! You don't have to do it but you can do it!!!" replied Centimuss.

Nat continued laughing. "When I designed him I had in these two entertainers in mind for his personality and voice. They were Soviet Womble and Exurb1a. Well these two entertainment persona… I took all of their videos and content that they have made over the years; all of the jokes they made, every single reference. They also helped in making him. So that is how I got this witty British companion. Currently his voice is a mixture of those two but normally he just chooses one of them. The manner in which he acts is from Soviet Womble and his tendency to science and philosophy and his political side is from Exurb1a; his witty behavior and British humor is from both of them. At first I gave him the name Phil but after a while he insisted on this name," Infinity explained.

"Why did you choose his personality like this?" asked Nat.

"Well....if I want to spend eternity with someone, I rather them having a British accent and to be funny. He could change his accent anytime he wants to but I figure he likes too," replied Infinity.

"Please stop! Nobody wants to listen to a birthing story!" exclaimed Centimuss,

"I need you!! You are literally the smartest being in the complete multi-verse," said Infinity.

"Oh please! You are flattering me. This is all going to go straight to my ego. Do please continue!" replied Centimuss.

"Just please stop processing one of those lifes," said Infinity.

"And mess up my reputation in the lives that I made? No sirrey!! Sorry, it is a stupid idea anyway," said Centimuss in bewilderment.

"Pretty please with a cherry on top. We have been here together from the beginning, I can't do it without you!" Infinity pleaded.

"Fine, okay! You're pulling my circuits!!" he mumbled to himself. Centimuss replied.

"God damn stupid apes, can't do anything for themselves" He said for the benefit of the others.

"Pardon me? Could you repeat that please," said Infinity.

"Oh it's nothing. I just said how effective and efficient you are that you can do your own jobs by yourself," chirped Centimuss happily.

"He actually said 'stupid apes that can't do anything for themselves'; do you not like humans?" asked Nat.

"Bit of a snitch aren't you? Well, it also appears that you do not appreciate sarcasm. No I have nothing against humans -- just stupid people and Sapiens species is filled with stupid people," replied Centimuss. He then made a :-) on the monitor.

Centimuss stopped the processing of a few of his bodies. One of the sidewalls opened and he started assembling a new robotic body for himself. He assembled it and activated the new body. It looked very human-like but was made out of metal and plastic. He started walking towards the door, stopped and looked back at them, saying: "Well come on then. What are you waiting for? A formal invitation? Let's giddy-up!"

Together they left the room, the doors closing silently behind them.

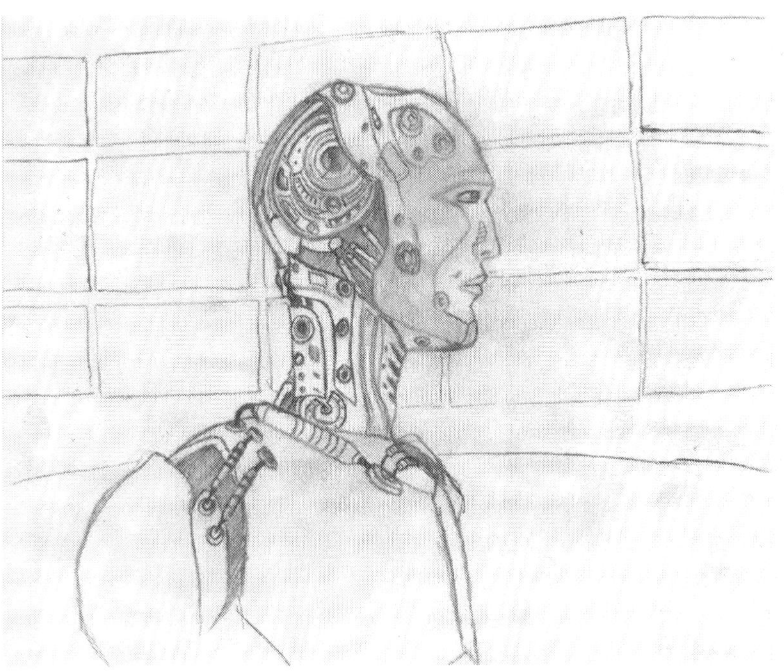

XXXVIII. The Old Crew

Centimuss, Nat and Infinity were all sitting in the living room.

"Who are we looking for?" asked Nat.

"The old crew," replied Infinity.

"And who exactly is in the old crew?" quizzed Nat.

"Jesus! Do you always ask so many questions? The old crew consists of Hero Key, Joy, Jim, Jack, Jenny, Jessica, Janet, Jake, Jon or as I like to call them "The group of people who insist upon the letter 'J' " or "The Jays" for short. The most important one of them all, is of course, me," Centimuss replied.

"Thank you for the explanation" Infinity said. Centimuss winked.

"By any chance do you know where any of them are?" Infinity asked Centimuss.

"I've been living with you all this time. I have no idea where they are but I will try to locate them" Centimuss replied.

Centimuss started processing and after a few moments, said "Most of them, well the ones that are still alive, have turned off their locators, all except one, which is specifically on our secret private signal. There is a note saying solar bar with a dimension address.

"Then I guess we should get moving, are you coming?" said Infinity.

"I actually have to finish lives that I have just started. I will end them abruptly, so I can have more processing power later on," said Centimuss.

"Okay then we will be leaving in 8 hours, with or without you. Nat, if you're hungry, get something to eat and then sleep. You won't have much chance of that for a while to come. And oh yeah when you meet them remember this...,"

Infinity then sang *heathens – twenty one pilots*.

"Okay," nodded Nat. She then stood up from the couch and went to the kitchen. She took out a medium-well-cooked steak out of the oven. She hadn't eaten a proper meal for days now and was ravished. She poured herself a soda and started eating the food and enjoying every single bite.

Centimuss went to his own room to give a proper and fitting end to his lives, so he could finally free up enough processing power so he could find the rest of the Old Crew.

Infinity went to the training room and started practicing, so that if he ever met Evil Key again he would have the upper hand. He did it all -- strength training, agility training, speed training, and combat training.

Around 7 hours later, Nat was still sleeping, Centimuss was living his lives having ended only sixty-nine percent of them. Infinity had just taken a shower and then headed to the entrance room and went to the second floor. He went to prepare something. He went into a room and turned on the lights.

XXXIX. The Solar Bar

The room was filled with an assortment of vehicles: bicycles, motorcycles, cars, chariots, warp-speed space crafts. He pressed a bottom and sent one of the spacecraft's to the entrance room. The spacecraft that was sent was red with a white stripe in the center. It resembled a Manta Ray. At the end of the wings, it had a white fiery artwork on it. It was obvious it was a fast spacecraft.

Infinity went to wake up Nat. He went to Nat's room and knocked on her door. She didn't wake up. Infinity starts banging on the door and still she didn't wake up, Infinity said to his ring "Activate, Wakey, Wakey in guestroom 23".

A scream could be heard from Nat's room. She opened the door, completely soaked, screaming in a rather pissed of tone: "If you EVER do that again, Evil keep beating your ass, will be the least of your worries!!" She grabbed a towel, drying herself off and they both went towards the entrance room.

As they entered into the room, Nat was shocked to see a spacecraft. She stood in at awe before it.

"She is such a beauty, but why do you have one? What is the point of having one?" asked Nat.

"Some places you can't open portals to and sometimes I just like to go out for a ride" replied Infinity sheepishly.

Infinity opened the cockpit of it and bowed: "After you, my Lady."

Nat went up into the cockpit with Infinity a few steps behind her. It was just one room, meaning, the cockpit, engine room, sitting room, storage room were all in one. The room wasn't very large but there were around 16 seats.

Infinity sat in the pilot's seat and Nat sat in the co-pilot's seat. Infinity flipped several switches and then opened a portal into which he flew the spacecraft at low speed into deep space. Infinity realized that he forgot to refill the energy tank. “Hey can you please give me that power battery I gave you, I’ll give you another one when we get back” he asked Nat. Nat gave him the solar battery and she asked: “It’s a warp ship, isn’t it?”

Infinity put the battery into a socket and it started draining the energy and replied: “Yes it is, how did you know?”

“My father has worked on the concept of this,” Nat replied.

“Do you know how it works?” Infinity asked as he was driving.

“If I recall correctly, it warps space and time in a way that makes us travel faster than light without being turned into energy,” Nat replied.

“Good job, I’m proud of you, but I got to ask, do you know how it does that?” Infinity said.

“No I don’t, but I would love to know!” Nat replied.

“There is going to be a controlled black hole in front of us, the energy that is being used, is to control the black hole so it does expand on us. We use the black hole’s gravitational force to bend space and time, whilst it also pulls us forward. In this manner we can easily go from one side of the universe to the other,” Infinity said.

“Warp speed is now accessible,” the ship's computer said.

“Are you ready? You know I am!” said Nat. “Great, just put on your seatbelt. There’s going to be some serious torque!!,” Infinity said.

Nat put on her seatbelt and so did Infinity, Infinity activated warp speed and they were pushed back into their seats with such force. A black hole, made in front of the ship began to drag them forcefully towards it. They could see everything around them was also being dragged along. By looking in front of them they could see the event horizon. Infinity put the ship on autopilot.

After a few more moments of looking out the windscreen and enjoying the view, Infinity said:" I'm going to make it go faster, at this rate we will reach the other side of the universe in 12 hours".

Infinity started singing *across the universe – Beatles* this song increased the speed of the ship. After the song ended Infinity took a nap, while Nat continued looking out the windscreen, the view around them being dragged even faster so that they could see the past. About an hour later they reached her destination. Nat poured a glass of water on Infinity waking him up with a slight touch of revenge. Infinity parked the ship into a crowded parking lot. They had reached the solar bar.

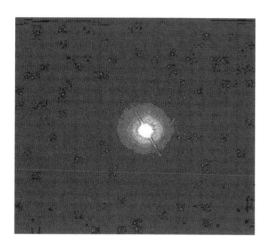

XL. Joy

Infinity and Nat entered into the bar. They went straight to the main bar and sat on the barstools. The bartender was organic. Infinity ordered some Japanese whiskey. They served him his drink. Infinity paid for his drink and said thank you. Infinity started sipping it and began looking around the bar. He noticed somebody sitting in the corner of the bar, talking to someone, a bluish reptilian with tentacles, with emerald green eyes.

"Do you see that person in the corner over there?" Infinity whispered to Nat.

"Yes, his eyes are so beautiful," Nat replied.

"He is a lantern!" Infinity replied.

"A lantern? Like Green Lantern from DC?" Nat replied.

"No child!! They are from the book Fifth Science. You should give it a read. It is a very interesting story. But something that is unique to them is they can tell the most probable future," Infinity replied.

"I figure you're looking for someone, mind if I asked who it is," the bartender interrupted them from behind.

"I am looking for Joy. She gave me the coordination's for this place, and she said she will be at Solar Bar, even though this place isn't named that," Infinity replied.

"Go to the bathroom and touch the mirror," the bartender said.

Infinity stood up from his stool and gulped down the rest of his drink and put a tip for the bartender. They both went to the bathroom door. There was only one unisex door. They both went inside. Infinity looked at the mirror and put his hand on. The mirror started scanning his hand and then a hidden door opened in one of the stalls. They both entered through it, going down a flight of stairs. They found themselves inside a hidden club underneath the bar above. There was music playing, the song *blind – Dayne S* could be heard.

Infinity noticed a VIP room on the other side of the room. They headed towards it. Infinity was a few steps ahead of Nat. As they were walking, somebody roughly grabbed Nat's wrist. It was a creature, with the body of the ogre and the head of a blobfish. It was bright yellow. There were more of them around the table but in different colors, such as brown and orange. "Come and sit with us! Have a drink" it said in a maleficent tone.

Nat pulled her wrist but he was gripping it tightly. "Thank you but no, I'm not thirsty,". The ogre didn't let go and insisted for her to sit down. Suddenly Infinity turned back and cut off the ogre's hand from the wrist with a sword. The creature pulled its arm back in pain. "Next time sword is going to go through your chest," Infinity protectively said.

Nat, noticeably shaken, started going ahead with Infinity close behind her. Nat opened up the hand gripping her wrist and dropped it to the floor. They reached the room in front of which stood a burly bodyguard by the door. Infinity asked "Joy's room?" The Bodyguard replied "Yes, but she isn't receiving anyone." Infinity played the message from Joy to him and he stood respectfully aside.

"You go in first. I think she may be angry to see me first," Infinity whispered to Nat.

Nat gulped and went in. In the room, which was dimly lit with orange lights, was a curved couch with a small table in front of it. In the middle, there was a woman sitting there. The woman was wearing leather Indiana Jones-style clothes. She wore the trademark leather hat and like Nat had one of those satchels. She also had one of those rings. She had purple hair with highlights in them. She held a glass in her hand although Nat couldn't quite make out what was in it. She was laying back on the couch, her legs crossed.

"The bartender said you were looking for me. He also said you were with another person," she said.

"Yes. He will be inside in a minute," Nat replied.

She took a sip from her drink and said: "Tell me what you want?"

"My friend and I were hoping you could help us," Nat replied.

She took another sip from her drink and asked: "And exactly who is your friend?"

Infinity came through the door and cheerfully said: "Hey Joy,"

"And who are you?" Joy asked.

Infinity raised his hand with his ring showing. Joy was shocked, she spilled her drink dropping the glass to floor. She put her hands against her hair and sang *oh my God – Jacqueline Irvine*.

Infinity came and sat down next to her on the couch. She instantly came and hugged him and then slapped him and continued hugging him. Infinity said "Oww." "I missed you, you big doof!!" Joy exclaimed. Infinity hugged her back.

She stopped hugging him and asked in an angry tone: "How come you came back to me? I thought you said that you never want to see any of us again".

"I didn't want to. I didn't want to put you all in danger again. I couldn't live with myself after their deaths. Imagine how horrible I would've felt if you had all died and it was all because of me. I love you all" Infinity replied.

"Dear, I love you as well" Joy replied, they both hugged again.

"How come you came back on then?" asked Joy.

Infinity nodded his head towards Nat.

"How do you want me to help?" Joy asked.

"Evil is hunting her down," Infinity replied.

Joy asked "Bloody Evil Key! You have gone mad! What makes her so special that you're risking your life for her?!?"

"I'm still right here you know," Nat replied. Joy gave her a strict look and Nat went silent.

Infinity sent Joy a mental message of the message James had sent him. After Joy reviewed it in her head, she looked up and just said: "Oh, that's why,"

She took a deep breath and said "As I said before I will always be by your side."

They all stood up went towards the door. Joy kicked Infinity in the nuts. Infinity bent over in pain.

"That is for making us leave you" Joy said.

They all want out the door and Joy noticed the creature whose hand Infinity had cut off sprawled unconscious on the floor.

"What happened here?" Joy asked.

The creature's colleagues started start explaining the preceding events from their point of view. Joy mentally checked the security cameras as they continued spinning their yarn. She saw exactly what happened.

"Oh I see the problem now. Let me deal with it right away!" she soothingly said to the Ogres.

She took out a laser blaster from her jacket and pointed it towards the person who had tried to harass Nat and shot him, killing him on the spot.

"Problem solved, goodbye gentleman," she waved.

The three of them left to the spacecraft and blasted off.

XLI. A Blast from the Past

The three of them were inside the spacecraft. Infinity and Joy were sitting in the pilot seats and Nat was sitting in the passenger seat to the left of Infinity. Infinity activated warp speed.

"Oh it's been so long I have not been in here. We used to go on so many adventures in here!" Joy sighed.

Infinity smiled, looking at her and said: "You always knew how to make a long ride fun, Joy."

Joy started singing *those were the days - Mary Hopkins*.Infinity and Nat enjoying her singing also joined in.

"So how you are? What's new with you?" Infinity asked.

"For a while I spent some time with the others but each of us found someone special that they decided to spend time with, that is everyone except me! I went exploring with them at first but when they all left, I was all alone. Nothing stopped me from me being me. I sometimes I went to other dimensions, made secret empires in those clubs/bars. Whichever universe I went to I always put it in our channel just in case you ever want to come, so you could locate me... and finally you have," Joy replied. "How about you, what's new with you?" asked Joy.

"Well after she died, I built her a memorial." He was cut off by Joy, who cried "Oh that was you then? It's so very beautiful. She would've been proud of you."

"I tried to get rid of Centimuss but he wouldn't leave, like malware, he invaded every single computer and device I had, so I just accepted him being there. He knew that if Evil Key would attack, he would be badly damaged. He also said he wanted to use the processors I have, as they are quite strong, and he wasn't normally active in the base," Infinity smiled.

"Damn it!! I should have done that," Joy said.

“Then I made that base that I always wanted to make,” Infinity chuckled.

“The one outside of the Multi-verse? Are we going there now?” Joy gleefully asked. Infinity nodded. “Congratulations!” Joy said.

“Back then I was reading a lot of books, watching shows, movies, playing video games, out exploring, training, and never stayed long in a dimension, so I wouldn’t grow attached to it and wouldn’t become a victim of Evil Key. Most of the time I was alone, until I met Nat. And now my worst fears have happened as she is now being hunted down by Evil Key,” Infinity continued.

After a few moments Infinity remembered to say “Oh, by the way, I changed my name to Infinity,”

“Her epitaph,” Joy replied in a sad tone.

“Wow, we have missed so much of each other’s lives,” Joy said.

They both started singing *everything has changed - Taylor Swift ft. ED Shreeran* while Nat sat there quietly, not saying a single word.

XLII. The Lost One

The ship finally reached a place that they could open up a portal and they immediately went back to the base.

“Welcome back!! Especially you, Joy!! The feeling I never have,” Centimuss said.

“Well if it isn’t the Brit with the Wit. It’s good to see you too,” Joy replied.

Nat and Infinity also bade their greetings and salutations as they headed into the living room together.

Centimuss was sitting there “Well, I finally stopped processing all of those lives, do you know how many people I had to disappoint with my sudden deathsssssss? A bloody hell of an amount, that’s how much!! You’d better appreciate this! Both of you!!”

“I do thank you, my dear friend. Anyway Joy said the rest are retired now?” Infinity replied.

“Yes they are either married and on their last lives or already dead. So you have to get other people to help, how about Wade? Or ...,” Joy said.

Infinity interrupted Joy and saying, “No they won’t accept. I’m sure of it.”

They three of them fell into thought until, and Infinity broke the silence by saying “Perhaps, we can ask Rust.”

Both Centimuss and Joy looked up in amazement? “What makes you think that you can find him?” Centimuss asked.

“Or even if you do that he will accept” Joy added.

“Exactly who is Rust?” Nat asked.

"He is me, well a version of me. I know he will accept because he is me and he will accept it for the same reason I accepted," Infinity replied.

"Okay even if you have the slightest chance of getting him on board? He is hiding so well even I can find him!" Centimuss said.

"Well back when Nat and I were looking for Evil Key. We saw him," Infinity replied.

"You found him and you didn't tell me?" Centimuss said exclaimed. In a fit of rage Centimuss tased Infinity with a Taser, electrifying him but not at with a severe voltage.

"Can you all please stop hurting me!! I'm getting tired of this! And who do you think killed me?" Infinity said in a frustrated tone.

"That cat fellow!" Centimuss replied.

"I still don't know who he is. Can somebody explain it to me, please," Nat asked.

"Remember me explaining that I and Evil Key used to be friends and we had a fight?" Infinity asked.

"Yes," said Nat.

"Well, the stuff that he saw, scarred him. And so that his consciousness could continue without the pain, and so he would not be miserable all the time, which he frankly was, he created a special consciousness. One, which prevented the other personalities to enter into his body and one which didn't transmit his memories to his main memory vault. He had a hidden vault somewhere else," Centimuss said.

"Apparently he knows something so important that he cannot die. Because he didn't want to have an identity crisis, he chose the identity Rust and we haven't heard of him since the genocide," Joy said.

"Well I'm off to go get him. Either he will join us or not," Infinity said.

Infinity stood up from the couch and walked towards the main hall.

"How do you know where he is?" Joy asked.

"I know I will find him because we are one," Infinity replied

Infinity started walking down the main hall into the entrance room, opened a portal and left. The portal closed behind him.

XLIII. The Broken Key

The three of them started talking after Infinity's departure.

"Joy, do you mind explaining to me what you are exactly, Infinity explained it only quite vaguely," Nat asked.

Joy chuckled and saying "Back when he just started and was learning how to fight, he was putting himself through hell. one of the things that he did was to sacrifice his mental health. He accepted something that he could not handle. Even before he accepted it, he already wasn't in great shape. It caused him PTSD. Post-Traumatic Stress Disorder. So he needed help to focus with the pain and to overcome it. And by pain I mean both mental and physical. He focused on the pain so much that I was created and a few days later the rest of us were made as well. Slowly but surely, we all made a part of his personality. I am one of the personalities who is generally loving and joyful and yet at times strict and serious. One is his own original personality. He wouldn't allow any of us to control his body, except on some rare occasions. For a long time, we were only in his head and our sole purpose was to take care of him and help him mentally and emotionally. After a time he started noticing we had been developing into our own persons and he himself felt bad of keeping us in his head, even though we didn't really mind it. He wanted to give us rights that we didn't know we wanted. He gave us our own bodies and our own servers, so we could store our memories, since the brain only had a limited capacity, and well you know the rest,"

"Oh how very interesting. How about you Centimuss?" Nat replied.

"Well you already have heard enough about me. All I can say is my purpose was to help Infinity and to be a companion to him. He secretly gave me free will. He let me decide what I wanted to be. One of the scariest things was to decide my own purpose but I appreciated it. I knew he needed me so I stayed with him later on. He doesn't know me as a machine; he knows me as a person. Yes, he might be irritating at times, but he's worth it. Unlike most humans," Centimuss replied.

"Oh by the way, *what is* your opinion on humans? I have noticed you are annoyed by them. Do you like us?" asked Nat.

"Besides them taking centuries to learn to not throw their feces around and spending around 2 to 3 years of their lives drooling, I like them. And I have even fallen in love with some of them. Oh except stupid ones, I bloody hate those ones. They could burn as far as I care. This goes for all species," Centimuss replied.

"Oh I'm relieved, in my world, there is always such a fear of AI's but some people like my dad say there is nothing to fear," Nat replied.

"Certainly, he is a man of higher taste," Centimuss replied.

"By the way how's Infinity always so certain?" Nat asked.

"To be honest I don't know. He just knows. That is a unique ability that only a few dimension hoppers have. Rust and Evil Key are other people that also have this ability as well. Also he never forgets anything and he can explain something right down to the very smallest detail." Joy replied.

"What about Infinity? What's his story?" Nat asked.

An old man's voice could be heard down from the main hallway bellowing: "That is his story to tell."

Centimuss and Joy looked startled. "Well I be damned, the bastard did it," Centimuss said.

"Where is he?" Nat asked.

XLIV. Wonder

A portal had opened onto a world where the genocide had occurred. Sitting on the edge of a crater was the old man from before. He was wearing a gray blazer with a pocket square inside of its front pocket, with dark blue colored jeans and smart brown suede shoes. Oxfords not Brogues. He had a beard and mustache and looked like an artist and his hair was long but well groomed. His hair and beard were gray with a few strains of black hair here and there. Unlike Infinity he did not have a ring. He looked like he was in his 70s going on80.

Infinity went and sat next to him and said: "wanderer, who are you? I see you going your way without scorn, without love, with unfathomable eyes, damp and sad, like a plumb line that has come back, unsatisfied from the depths into the light. What were you looking for down there? With a breast that does not sigh, with lip that hide its disgust, with hands that now grasp only weakly, who are you? What have you been doing? Have a rest here, this place is hospitable to everyone. Relax and whoever you happen to be, what would you like now? What do you need to recuperate, just name it! What I have I will offer you for relaxation. Recuperation? Oh, you inquisitive man, what are you talking about? Tell me what you beg for? What? Just say it! One more mask? A second mask?"

"Fredrick Nietzsche, beyond Good and Evil; when Eternity is at your step, you have a lot of time to read," he replied softly.

"I thought we didn't like having beards?" Infinity said with a smile.

"I still don't, I'm just not bothered to shave it," the old man replied.

"I never got to thank you for ...," Infinity replied.

He was cut abruptly by him, Rust saying "You never needed to, cut to the chase. I already know why you are here."

"Then you already know why I need your help. The reason you've been staying alive all these years...," Infinity replied.

"I stayed alive because I wanted to, even though everything is gloomy and sad for me," he replied.

"Hell if my state is this bad, I can't imagine yours," Infinity replied.

"What were you doing all this time?" asked Infinity.

"I don't like talking about the past," replied Rust.

After a few moments of silence and the sound of wind passing by, Rust said "What you're about to do is very stupid, you know?"

"I know" replied Infinity.

"You're most probably going to get killed," said Rust.

"I know but you would do the same," replied Infinity looking at him. "Please consider it."

Rust started singing *Hopeless wanderer – Mumford and sons* while Infinity's ring glowed.

"I have to go and finish what I've started," said Rust standing up.

Infinity gave him a key to a room.

He stood up, opened a portal and left, the portal closing behind him.

Leaving Infinity sitting there at the crater's edge.

XLV. The New Crew

As Infinity stood up he accidentally he slipped and fell into the crater. He stood up and dusted himself off. He opened a portal and went through it, the portal closing behind him.

He entered into the entrance foyer and headed down the main hall into the living room. Looking to the left, at the dimensions. He was walking quite slow and very cinematically.

He finally reached the living room where he saw everybody there, including Rust, who was leaning against the counter of the kitchen.

"Thank you" Infinity said to Rust.

Rust nodded back.

Infinity then said to them "I know a lot of you have sacrificed much for me and I want to thank you all. Alone we are weak but together we are strong. Just like the Old Crew was. We are now the New Crew. We are the people lost in infinity. I was never good with pep talks but I know the perfect song for this occasion,"

Infinity started singing *3 foot tall – classified*and everyone started singing with him in harmony.

After the song, Infinity said "We have to plan what we're going to do next. Centimuss can you please encode your most challenging encryption please"

"Okay, anybody trying to attempt to crack this, I am sorry," Centimuss said.

The base started a count-down: "24-hour long encryption activated in 3... 2... 1...

13-5 17-21-9-20 13-25 23-8-9-14-9-14-7 9 3-1-14 6-5-5-12 13-25 4-9-13-5-14-19-9-15-14-19 7-5-20-20-9-14-7 19-20-18-9-16-16-5-4 1-23-1-25

XLVI. Good Luck

QORXYN XWDVIO IHWMYL RIZWNI ZHGKGO ZZXIBH HQQZQR SEDWQY
GYHWDE TJINTA WFXUXD CMLJDP NRDKNY BLDGNO ZHVEKT FQSERL
ITWMDX WCHDUV ZZFBBK WDJDVU GLFAEH LCBLYH FGDTDU ASLCRE
SWJRGP IZTNPW DVSPWB MPUZAU GLEMMU BUFJME CUFBOP
HDBVAH MNDXXL PAPAAU YJXAMS XCMPGH HLRMPL SVRDST YKBSOA
UNEBLD KVTBBA SVUUTR XSPZAY QXEWWV COHVXL BNKNGX PQHPRS
LGEYUZ VGAINI TFFECC JGFCOJ UCYWZG JKGBVC HVXGWX WVPJGM
XOYFPO KLPFXS WLEMFT NOHCSU YUICNH RWUOFA XOZRIM PRTWZP
XUPNLU JZYJPT SNPVWZ OYIFVA ULSSJB WUWQDP YUCOVO DTFGKP
FQXONP WZQAPC XBUYZL UUIYYM XOXFPQ OFLOKC CKJWOS ILVNPU
DPDRSZ SRLNJS JWCFYZ DALNHI RMYJRR AGJRPX SJQMZQ NWTWEG
WFQNWZ NWEBPX AQAXFB MPURBF KJXELO HOJNFQ KYQVZY NOAROD
YDQXPO NEYCUH QKOILZ RQQQKY YCVKNO WXMLDI RHRTMD HZTOBF
GPJOJG YBRVAF POPDEW JLYZPV SKJWDG JUPDZH ZSAPAD UBOKPI
TTBQYI LATQKO TZNLFB GGJXZI AVCDUL DLMBGK AUBLEE AYXPIO
ZUVSPW TCAWYI WWBDWJ IYPEAF JWZCXB KFECGM EKGQZN EUSIGB
ZOEJDC HWMDNA OYQJYV KRNQTO RQBLJX ZWATJI DHREFN FQAPFL
OMPOUB JFRWOE KCVSHR CEFWPT EYAOSO TELAOK NBPFDG FSMQBU
ECLFGI UMUOTC IPUQLQ SRALFM VQFGJY MWHFDF ZLRJMC CZBZDB
CLRXPK NGJNXA LZXSJT UOKUAS IIZTAT JUYCDX TSGDQR IXZBKO
UDCOLE QKXXZO OYWKSX CILLDU FOBLBV LXQSKH LSJOHH WOQVKH
FPXLHO PRABWU FMVVFI QPIFJO LUESPG QERTGG JHMWWL TNNWLI
PWHEVO VYTLTY LKYPFZ KEGUJD SAXAKC OMWZVG SNYSHJ DMMDAI
ITDORW LGDPXG IDKESX UTVYQS MNKUOR YKLXIV BEVVWO XPXFHX
FZTWPV KCTPLH KZQTNE QTGWZN EJJQYI UMUWXS WBKOZO QHGHOB
HBWWQK LAIQCS HUYUYH ZHCKCX VQYKRJ NLDSAD LWGVDR JEYEYL
LGGUYP ABGEFV BAVWLJ NVGVRV YGGJRZ UVNOKR UDRKHU OMRRYU
DQAXNF OUREDG GUNJUE JSYUDE PZEWZD QRPZIA FEYRGF SCIGSR
JFVYHP NXZURA IXDWYH HZKYUO BXBQEI KNUGNM XNGGIU LKALKR
XDKGKG AFVWWZ LUWGGX LHEAUB YTUQIA SPKBKC GPWMUP JEHKHG

KYCYIY XMFWKH AILVHT KDZXWR HBTSRS CUQLXR EPCNBE DIPQOI
EJHQUT CCXEXC LBEENN HYELID IKIPKN VRBAXX XMWKBE FYQMZT
CWNXRX LOXVPB ORRUTL EKMXTE FMRHEQ NVGQWM FRCMSU
HUQUNJ UNWMLN TUHTOF EQLSXQ ZMTEHF HKCYIK ORCMXR
XWLGQH ZLBITS CQYSCN BZGJUU FHLZCJ EUNDOI KLKYRC TUWBCQ
GDUIQV TNXPQW XPHPUE YEHSIY JQAFUS JQRSEP PHIXLF OMZGWF
UXJQMK MPDQJR XYZUAI NODUVT YWVXOO ZWHMBI TUTGMD
TJTPWZ GSEFQW EDFFOD PLDOPI TGQHKC RMHPRU TKXVHQ VMFWZC
HFZLIE SCHSFN UBRBFQ KXZXLI RSJUJD ZVIKSW RPAQKN FNLWKN
RBBWDI RHAACM MAKKFP CCNMON WNZSQJ WNKYFZ BZVHJR SJGCUL
YBAPTU BZBZLY KXMFKA VZCSIP OKAEPH GXXHYP VCYJPK EIDHOC
XCBDGW VIKWJH NJHUBQ DSWTJZ ARLKIL LLGEWI TXWROL ZYDMLH
FJPDDY CJVWZW NBCDWS TCHXUW SOZTJK ZEIGNV VIOQPU NBLLJY
VXLOGU ASPOIV UBCZOL AJXDYL FMALVW ZWSKZE FVPCVB YHBEXG
YMORBS NTWDZN GUEVSS ITQQOQ MDUHHR GPMHCV XTLHMB
WXEOJD FCEANM EVYJWJ QIXKVU ECPJJI EIUMNY NPKTKQ CZKTMV
HJSYJZ MOMCNR JKQOSL FCWYOU KXSBWO LKWPFU HZDHUA PPGIJB
HQZHXN PGLMUM AMBYAJ VOEVSL ZXHREB ALLDPA JOIASS CYFQBH
IFZHXP TXWZJD FSZOEC KYAIIR HRKYDU KFYSUB RZYQOF UVAESZ
YPCMMC YWSVZU ADAYWL HIIOAB XHUFGD JPUKKR BDPZYG LKBCUF
LZNNVP ERAQHQ EVPDCT CXJUSR PYZEFU IYJZMH WCCILG TNHBMS
IPXNGS PUUXQK EQFDJQ MMSWDB LCTHXX INPMSF JHCYBL FNZVND
WSBAXI FSPJPB CDTLWD JTMVCC SICCVY QOHCWD UWZTRI ZBNKYQ
JOXCFQ HPTCTM ZZNRHJ HQUZLG PXQVVI VKUFII CFQGSP LXJUEL
KPBWAU GWGWXN MFHJTQ GJYGMK XYJMQI KJYHIN JQNOPX OBBGGO
VWFQJG WZIFMX UZMYVL VOBSQB QASONZ GHDRLQ TNABDK JJFENS
LSMVKI HHHHYY QKZGJP BWLPQX MEXIUM LFBCDI HVRLVE WPFJUP
ZUTRPB DNFQHH HKQJQM PXRGSB INUBJN NHVWAD RKWGVP
OXENMK VPFDGN QRGAZS HURHHX EMRCMR JHAFIC REUNLX OECSDW
OLEGPQ UKWHBU PTJMAR KBBCKZ AJDXMW XALZDS QDPLHA EYMFRO
OYUWNG TCWWLX MTLGDJ DYJNDU JYJITQ PPVYKU LAGRTI LQFKIN
KBFXZX OGWRPE USDISO GMOMXQ BQNUGE XCIMAR OCXXJD UWOPJC
RZMRMU OOIWTR VTYLCF XJHTWV HSSBQM YWGIEM ZTXKSM ZUOVPO
XUDZWX HPKDGB XJIDBQ VKUSVC CQNITG PHSCAR CVEXTJ NCTPRI
HHVVXR PHGARJ MBVLVH LOMZFM SYZBDT PILTFB RCTUUM OQYPWC

KDABMC GDRVJO AZBHKB WJCVFE PKRELJ SZPXUK JXURRS IMFVKI
CSBJCB NBDSGY OXURTZ GJCJVN TVBSYN AGGYQG CWKPVR XUEPLI
QIRJNB IVUOQN ERPLDT ZOPIKK ALRLKT JJQYSE PVFUBZ SYWHQC
HHCRPP KMUXCT EOIJQT PYIJIC OOHINN FKXTSF SMAVUX YWFGXR
PMDMTX ZACQDF VDHRUC IKEGBU WHRRDP QCDOEX BYRDCI UYJOFV
WQIERL CCMMLE PRNKWT GRVABS AOKUTY ODJJZT TDPLCB FAOIVM
AKIWQS MEJAPV JNONZJ USUCJG SFWWBD UHXKVG NTIBSY OZDJJI
JPKMXL AVVBDD ZTWQGD UBKXSC DSVQLZ QDRTON MZQDGB XUVLAX
EQBTZI NXODZL ZEPQSR JVTITL DVMUUL ZHECGR OZDRQG XMBIQT
XFMLAY AFHCZI UMQMOK GUCATE ILFGDT CJOLZU ZWPITT BAMGKD
VUVJMK ILWCYX UPPIJD DZENHO PFDWKV RZXCCP ZNOORP SAIJMO
NKONJF CAAYFC JUTCSW IDWWVT VKPJSB EEGAET LAULOA EDNQEP
UCGXMA VEEPNJ FMIQKO DAXBZN KVGQJW OFLBRQ BXENFO PWJPEZ
QATSBV YBOFHZ SWMKHB JENYZU BSDZYF VGKZHM IPCICN RQMOAT
TQSAYJ HQPMCB ZQVARW WPZZMA TIGUSG PSZSXL ZDCOPG TWVEXP
QRTRTZ JGJBMI HLTVLJ BIWVFL PXXGMO YCZRIY ILQFVY WSJQEL
PGUQXC ZRIKWT TUYLNC UJNRSW ENGDPM WKNKIV ZAPXYH CWCRQW
LFKZHH LNCIQB ZLAMJS QHSPHQ RIGSIO SLRXXI LBNHAP NMERBF
GBFJMQ QVFCYA WHKDYB RTINSZ AQVBXR VAVMVI XGBBTK HQTEHW
IILJJF ZNSUSO XPQQHN SWSFFX WBRFYX TQTIDZ OJFUPB EQDMUW
LECWND HMFJEF FSSURC PWIGIS IQWHLE BTPZCB VSQHZY PVAWRH
SDHAQM LYKTKB PNAFJG FHHFOQ NDCIXE EFOPSW BDLDRD QITLXL
RFBIVP NPXUHW FAIOSQ PKXKRX XSXVIY MYAEIH QMOMRL IBMOUI
LLWPPK OKHVRG MRYTPD PQNKFB RMWICX URYSSH XBAXKP JAQTAT
CCEVYB YVROER HFFGQL TVCETP QYFUBD VLGPPB MJSPNI WLPPMJ
UDPIIO ZJRWRC JPVYGG OZALQA TOKWMR GVRORB UTNVSU FUDNCE
NOEUKO KHJSUF EGYAUQ KMITVM QUZYUS WJOSFK IDVWKY NHPUGW
LNCWLU DBDBIZ OFMPDR NCOXQE LNCZNF GKFCFX GXNWTA AWXEXB
SOWDML LICRAL YDGAAO XPTRZN LXHZFX XHTQJY MUYEZP LMJUHW
TEXYZV SKXATU HGGZHR WCLPKZ IJBJYL SBMKRQ TNMXAK IPPUXM
LDBZHL SDHRUE LOGAER TCPMJP PNXGSQ XIAUCD SLFGIL VUVZPK
FIRFYE PMETVS UQJOQJ SDRSDA ASHCTZ LOEGMP KXEUYS FJPUTL
OYUMTY JFHOWQ BEUVZW XJEZNW QLYBGR QIUTTT XMCBVL XTJZJD
TAGAUS YABMID VKDBTB XCKOQN TGOYCX ZQXWKA HXRHGK SYIFYS
FJUSGO NQFTKA KTEKZF CRGVHN FRTHWX ANWVCU XYMHTX NXNURT

OLFPST DAGTNX CNPEHP VXTFOB MGRURM QKJKEL CLRBPJ NJKXXX MQALCU PXUY

3... 2... 1...

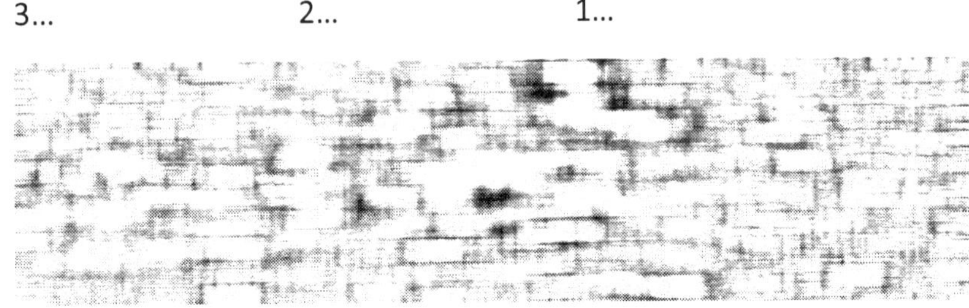

回来他现在没有什么可失去的，不像我，

你是对的，我没有什么可失去**的**

XLVII. Catching up

Portal opened and Infinity and Joy came out into the ruins of the old Key Empire.

"We should place some booby-traps. He will be expecting them but he won't know where the locations are going to be and those he knows he may forget in the middle of the fight," Infinity said.

They started placing and planting the booby-traps, some to blind Evil Key some to stun him.

"Be careful he doesn't hit you in the head, especially with a device. It could be a mind scrambler... and please don't die," Infinity said to Joy, as he placed a booby-trap.

"Duly noted," said Joy.

After they planted the remainder of the booby-traps on every conceivable track, they sat on one of the ruins next to each other.

They started talking: "About Nat, what do you think her real name is?" Joy asked.

"You know we can't talk about people's names," Infinity replied.

"You could always send a mental message," Joy said.

He sent her a mental message revealing Nat's true name to her.

Joy looked up and said: "Oh, how sweet."

After a few moments, Joy said: "You're pretty calm, I thought you would be scared."

"Scared is an understatement. I am terrified," Infinity replied.

“You sure do love her. She will be glad to have someone like you to watch over her,” Joy replied.

After a few more minutes, Joy asked: “So what is going to happen to me?”

“You know about the paradox. If I say it, it will be set in stone,” Infinity replied.

“Yes but I also know about the exceptions it has. Tell me,” Joy insisted.

They both sang *Acting up – G-Eazy ft. Devon Baldwin*

“I’ll give you an option to come back. Please accept it,” Infinity replied.

Joy hugged Infinity.

“How’s it going to end for you?” she asked.

Infinity replied with the song *wake me up – Avicii*. Joy hugged him even harder.

A robotic glitched out voice hissed from behind them: “Am I interrupting something? Too bad!”

XLVIII. Careful wishing

Evil Key blasted towards Infinity and Joy. Both of them dodged the blasts.

"It looks like you brought a friend, since you couldn't defeat me last time! How are you Joy? I was wondering where you were. I thought he abandoned you all!" Evil Key said.

Joy took out her blaster and start shooting at him. "I never fell for any of your mind tricks before, so just quit it," she said.

Evil Key dodged the blasts but then got shot from behind by one of the Taser trap. While he was being electrified he cried "Really! Traps!" Infinity seeing the opportunity hit him across the face, cracking the screen of his mask.

Evil Key fell to the ground. On his knees and he looked up at Infinity, his face glitching out and cried out: "For that, I will make you suffer more.".

Evil Key hurled one of the blocks of ruins at Infinity but Joy used her ring to deflect it in another direction.

Evil Key and Infinity began wrestling each other in hand-to-hand combat. This time Infinity was more prepared and he was getting more hits in, when Joy also came into the combat. Evil Key was so overwhelmed by their attack that he couldn't get any punches through.

Out of frustration Evil Key made an explosion between the three of them, hurling each of them in different directions.

Evil Key landed on another booby-trap temporarily blinding him for only a few seconds, enough time for him to trip over another trap which shot an arrow through his calf. His mask made an agonized and angry expression.

He groaned in pain. He started singing * ... Ready for it? - Taylor Swift* which caused a wave of distortion waves to deactivate all of the remaining booby-traps. The distortion waves also stopped the rings from working properly as well as Joy's blaster. Their clothes reverted back to their default defenseless form.

Evil Key then rejoined the hand-to-hand combat with Infinity and Joy, even singing while doing so. His leg that was wounded caused him from not doing some moves but still he managed to fend off those two. He suddenly saw an opening and hit Joy in the head with a device. She fell and started having a seizure. Infinity saw her like that and kicked Evil Key in the knee of his wounded calf, breaking Evil Key's leg. Evil Key staggered back, tripped over some rubble and fell.

Infinity rushed to take the device off of her head. Evil Key charged into his side causing them both to tumble to the ground. Infinity instantly rolled over and stood up, as did Evil Key but in pain.

Infinity started singing *sweet dreams – Eurythmics* He received a boost in speed and strength, whilst also giving Evil Key distorted vision and hearing. Infinity was winning the fight and at the end, he took his ring, shooting Evil Key in both of his shoulders and his knees. This made Evil Key lose the ability to move his arm and legs. He then broke Evil Key's finger that wore the ring and threw it side, making Evil Key unable to use it. Hitting him once more in the head, he causing Evil Key's mask to fly off.

XLIX. No Joy in loss

Infinity went towards Joy. The device was a mind scrambler which corrupts the mind and memories. It also had a needle which could be fatal.

Infinity picked her up and put her in her arms saying in a very worried tone: "No, no, no!! I told you to be careful." Infinity instantly called Centimuss, Infinity said to him "How much longer is left?"

"10 minutes left," Centimuss replied.

"Do it faster please!!" Infinity replied.

"I'm already doing it as fast as I can. it is a bloody quantum computer you know!" Centimuss replied.

Infinity quickly started singing * life and her yet – Rag'n'Bone *. The song started uncorrupting and Saving Joy's mind that were stored in her head. It also helped to recuperate and heal her.

Thankfully, Joy gained consciousness and started rubbing her head where the needle had pierced. "How am I still alive? I felt my mind being wiped clean," she said. She began to remember and said: "Is he neutralized? Did we get him?" Infinity hugged her and said "This is why I asked you to leave, see. So you wouldn't suffer like you just did," she embraced his hug.

Laughing could be heard, it was Evil Key. "Congratulations!! You saved her and defeated me. It Only took you an ocean of booby-traps and risking a loved one's life. You really are stupid. Is this supposed to stop me or something. I'll just die and get another body, and come after you , slowly but surely torture every single person you care about... even the slightest bit. Toodaloo!"

Evil Key started bashing his head continuously against a sharp side of a rock. Infinity went to stop him but he was too late, Evil Key had killed himself. His ring flew off his hand picking up all of his possessions along the way and opened a portal and left. The portal closed behind it.

Infinity instantly called Rust and said, "Be ready!! He's coming!"

Joy and Infinity opened a portal and went back to their own base.

L. Wise words

A portal opened and Nat, Rust, and Centimuss came out of it. They were inside Evil Key's base. Looked like any other base, except it was a spaceship in an empty universe. It seemed to be empty. They were in an entrance room. Everything was going well, until the defense system was activated.

Nat's shield protected them but it was taking a lot of damage. They walked towards one of the computers. Centimuss touched it and start hacking the normal defense AI. He was successful. He had now gained control of the defense system of Evil Key's base. He then quickly downloaded and reviewed the schematics of the base.

"What about taking a little bit of a detour? Let's first go to the power room. We should be able to lay some booby-traps there in case he comes in and we have to leave in a hurry. His base will be gone in the blink of an eye. What do you say chaps?" Centimuss said.

"I agree, it is always good to have a backup plan," Rust said.

"What about Infinity's plan?" Nat said.

"He already knows about the change in the plans or he would've not warned us," Centimuss replied.

"Okay then, lead the way," Nat said.

They all followed Centimuss. He went into the elevator as did the others.

"We exactly have three minutes to plant these, so don't waste any time you rascals!" said Centimuss

As elevator door opened they all ran towards the power room and opening the door they all rushed in.

The room was filled with solar batteries, hundreds of them, all powering his base. In the middle stood a black hole generator which was harnessing the gravitational force of two controlled black holes and converting it into energy.

Centimuss looked at the black hole generator and said: “Oh this is going be great!” He threw a bunch of explosives to Nat and Rust. “Plant these at the weak points that you notice. Also don’t pile them up, and try to scatter them.” The three of them started planting the explosives and the quickly went out of the room and headed into the server room, which contained Evil Keys consciousness and memories.

“Keep a lookout, will you? It’s going to take all my processing power and I can’t be risked being distracted. And no to you Nat, before you ask, I am not just bashing buttons, I am fighting with a computer that is speeded instantly. Luckily my own processors are also quantum,” Centimuss said.

“I know what a quantum computer is!! We also have those in my dimension,” Nat replied in an offended voice.

“shshshshshshshshshshshshshsh child. What did I just say about distraction! And if you two are going to keep on talking, keep it down” Centimuss ordered.

Centimuss started to hack the computer, Nat and Rust standing next to him, providing protection.

Only a few moments passed before Rust said to Nat: “He really cares about you, you know!”

“What? Who?” Nat replied.

“You know, Infinity. I can even say he loves you,” Rust replied.

“I did overhear him speaking with somebody. She asked him if he had a crush on me and he replied no. So what makes you think that you are correct?” Nat asked.

"Well, what did she asked next?" Rust replied.

"She asked what the singing was about. It was obvious, it was about love. He replied he loves me but not in that way," Nat replied.

"Well what do you think that meant?" Rust replied.

"I don't know, as a friend, perhaps?" Nat replied.

"Nobody risks their life for a friend they have met only recently!" Rust replied.

After a few moments, Rust said "You have a lot of things to learn, still. I just hope that experience is not your teacher, instead of Infinity. Also mostly, I hope you survive!"

Nat chuckled and said, "Thank you! We appreciate you being here!"

After a few moments passed Nat spoke again: "So Evil Key used to be your friend?"

"Yes, he used to be that person, but he is no longer that person," Rust replied.

"Have you ever tried to give him redemption?" Nat asked.

"Have you ever considered giving Hitler a second chance?" Rust replied.

"But wasn't he your friend? Don't you care about him?" Nat asked.

"Care about him? I gave him everything in my power to keep him happy, to keep him from becoming this monster. I looked at him as an equal. There are not that many people that I can say that for!" Rust replied.

Rust sighed and said: "Everything I did to keep him from becoming this person, failed. I could not stop him from becoming the way that he thinks. I couldn't stop him, from him accepting to be his own shadow. I did my part. He is the one that decided not to do his part."

"So he didn't want to be saved. A tragic story that is set in time?" asked Nat.

"I go on every day, wishing that I could've saved him. Wishing the genocide didn't happen. Wishing that Evil Key wasn't created. But all of those were just wishes. Good intentions but it has no final value," Rust replied.

"By the way, what was the reason that you made this special body, without the others?" Nat asked.

"I don't like talking about it," Rust replied.

"Okay, I won't bother you with those questions," Nat replied.

"I'm very proud of Infinity. It is obvious that he has properly taught you," Rust replied.

"Thanks, I guess," Nat replied.

They both laughed. Rust asked about Nat's past history for a while and Nat filled him in.

Suddenly Infinity called out to Centimuss.

LI. In the Lions' Den

"How much longer is left?" Infinity asked Centimuss via the ring.

"10 minutes," Centimuss replied

"Do It Faster Please," Infinity replied.

"I'm already doing it as fast as I can, it is a bloody quantum computer you know!" Centimuss replied.

Rust and Nat overheard them. They went outside the room preparing some more booby-traps in the possible hallways he could come from. They set up some smoke traps and stun traps. They also set the elevator in the right position.

Infinity called Rust and said, "Be ready he is coming!"

"Be ready in flight mode. You're going to have to bring us down," Rust said to Nat.

They were there for about another 2 minutes when Centimuss said: "Okie Dokey! I 'm done. Let's go!"

As they were walking down the hallway to the elevator, Centimuss was monitoring the security system where he noticed a ring coming from the entrance Pad and up the elevator shaft going through the elevator. When the elevator's doors opened the ring came out through its doors but there was no elevator. The ring swept behind them to the other side of the hallway where Evil Key was standing with his hands raised. The ring flew onto his finger and his mask was back, the rest of his outfit also reforming. His mask was still broken from the previous fight and still had the angry expression on it.

He took a step forward activating a smoke trap and a stun trap in synch.

Rust through grenade and held on to Nat, Centimuss also holding on to her as well. She flew down the elevator shaft and landed onto the floor they were going to and broke through the doors. They started running for all their lives were worth. the sound of another explosion could be heard from upstairs. Centimuss was using Evil Key's own defense system against him. Even so, Evil Key was going through them like a knife through butter. He then broke through the floors reaching them. Rust fired at Evil Key but he was protected by his outfit and didn't receive much damage.

Nat went back into flying mode, picking both of them up. As she was flying, she was going faster and faster to the point where it was hard for Evil Key to catch up with them but which still did not put enough distance between them. Centimuss detached his body to the stage that he only retained his head. His body parts exploded behind them, slowing Evil Key further down and giving them the distance they needed.

They're were getting close to the portal pad.

Rust threw a puff grenade. It exploded and made a puffy semi-hard substance fill up the hallway. He then took out his portal gun and shot it opening a portal to another dimension.

From that point on Nat and Rust were running. Nat holding Centimuss' head tight to her bosom.

Centimuss was yelling: "Run faster! Faster, I say! I would say imagine you're being chased by a hound but you're being chased by something much worse."

Nat was ahead of Rust...

Nat went inside the portal first. They entered into a rather ordinary looking dimension. The portal was by a beach with palm trees all around. But the color scheme was all different. Instead of being green leaves with brown trunks it was purple leaves with orange wood. The sand was also black instead of beige. The water was pink instead of blue. Rust stood before entering back into the portal "Goodbye, it was an honor!"

Rust closed the portal. Nat ran back to the place the portal was and cried out "No! No! No! Why did you do that? Why did he do that Centimuss?"

"So he could save us. Come on let's go home, dear," Centimuss replied.

"Is he going to come back?" asked Nat.

"I doubt it. Let's get out of here," said Centimuss.

Nat started singing *dream - imagine Dragons* a portal opened taking them straight to the base. They went through the portal and the portal close behind them.

On the other side Infinity and Joy were waiting. When Nat came out of the portal. Infinity rushed and hugged her. There were tears coming down her face.

"I know, I know. He did it because he cares about you" Infinity said.

Nat was just crying and hugging Infinity back. Joy was also quite and sad about Rust.

Joy took Centimuss' head and put it in one of the sockets. Centimuss pulled his head through the wall and the wall closed after it. After a few moments, he came back with another flashier body.

"Well, isn't this dapper. Let's get a move on. Shall we, chaps," said Centimuss, trying to cope with his grief.

"Why aren't you sad? I thought you said you adored him!" Nat yelled at Centimuss.

Centimuss replied in an insulted and somewhat aggressive tone: "Sad? I am sorrowed. I'm heartbroken. But what's the point to cry about it. He willingly gave his life so we can have ours! So don't try to lecture me about this. Also, I'm British and I don't show my emotions. That's why I was so easy for Infinity to make me. I just resort to humor,"

"I am sorry," Nat replied.

"You better be," Centimuss said.

LII. Wilting

"So what now?" asked Nat.

"We first activate the Rose virus, then we activate those explosives that Centimuss said to plant," said Infinity.

"And that's why you should never doubt what I say," said Centimuss.

"What is the Rose virus?" asked Nat.

"It is a killer virus for me that Centimuss made. It changes then corrupts then deletes files, making them completely unrecoverable. Afterwards, it causes the computer and servers to burn," explained Infinity.

"It also spams the computer so much that not even a quantum computer can handle it. You can compare it to taking a Ferrari and making it look like a snail-drawn cart!! You can't use the computer anymore because of so many pop-ups of a wilting Rose," continued Centimuss.

"Oh so that's where it gets its name from. Please activate it now. I want him to pay!" demanded Nat.

Infinity started singing * Roses - The Chainsmokers ft. Rozes * activating the Rose virus that they have planted in the computers and servers.

Instantly all the computers and screens at Evil Keys base started bringing up countless millions of pop-ups of Rose petals falling off and it's slowly wilting as the monitors and screens showed:

```
WWWWWWWWWWWWWWWWWWWWWWWWWWWWWWWWWWWWWWWWWWW
WWWWWWWWWWWWWWWWWWWWWWWWWWWWWWWWWWWWWWWWWWW
WWWWWWWWWWWWWWWWWWWWWWWWWWWWWWWWWWWWWWWWWWW
WWWWWWWWWWWWWWWWWWWWWWWWWWWWWWWWWWWWWWWWWWW
WWWWWWWWWWWWWWWWWWWWWWWWWWWWWWWWWWWWWWWWWWW
WWWWWWWWWWWWWWWWXOKWWWWWWXXWWWWWWWWWWWWWWWW
WWWWWWWWWWWNK0Oxl;:dOOkxdllodx0NWWWWWWWWWWW
WWWWWWWWWWNxc:::;'.,,,.',,',,,;dXWWWWWWWWWW
WWWWWWWWWNkc::::;',;,,''''.,;;,lKWWWWWWWWWW
WWWWWWWWWNd;;,;;;,;,'....''',',xNNWWWWWWWWW
WWWWWWWWWXd;::;;;;;,,',,',,;;,'lKNNWWWWWWWW
WWWWWWWWWXd:cc:,;:;,:cc:,,,,,;,,cONNWWWWWWW
WWWWWWWWWXo:cccc:::c::;;,,;;,,,'cKNWWWWWWW
WWWWWWWWWXxc:cclc:::;,,,,;;;;;'',dNWWWWWWWW
WWWWWWWWWWN0dlclc,,,,,,,,,,,,''',oKWWWWWWWW
WWWWWWWWWWWWNOdl;;cc:::,.....:x0NWWWWWWWWWW
WWWWWWWWWWWWWNKxddxxdc;;;;:cxKNWWWWWWWWWWWW
WWWWWWWWWWWWWWNNNKxxKXXXNWWWWWWWWWWWWWWWWWW
WWWWWWWWWWWWWWWWWWWWNKkkNWWWWMWWWWWWWWWWWWW
WWWWWWWWWWWWWWWWWWWWX0xONWWWWWWWWWWWWWWWWWW
WWWWWWWWWWWWWWWWWWWWX0xOWWWWWWWWWWWWWWWWWWW
WWWWWWWWWWWWWWWWWWWWX0xx0OxdodkKXNWWWWWWWWW
WWWWWWWWWWWWWWWWWWWMXOdooc;,,,;cldKWWWWWWWW
WWWWWWWWWWWWWWWWWWWWKOo:clc;;;;;;c0WWWWWWWW
WWWWWWWWWWWWWWWWWWWWKdl;;colcc::;lKWWWWWWWW
WWWWWWWWWWWWWWWWWWWWOldxllxkdooocxXNWWWWWWW
WWWWWWWWWWWWWWWWWWWWNkckXOO0OkxxxdkXXNWWWWWW
```

```
XXNNNNNNNNNNNNNNNNNNNNNNNNNNNNNNNNNNXXXXXXX
NNNNNNNNNNNNNNNNNNNNNNNNNNNNNNNNNNNNNXXXXXX
NNNNNNNNWWWWWWWWWWWWWWWWWWWWNNNNNNNNNNNNXXX
NNNNWWWWWWWWWWWWWWWWWWWWWWWWWWWWNNNNNNNNNNN
NNWWWWWWWWWWWWWWWWWWWWWWWWWWWWWWWWNNNNNNNNN
WWWWWWWWWWWWWWNkONWWWWWWXO0XXNWWWWWWWWWWNNNNNN
WWWWWWWWWWWNXOl;;lxkxddc',::ckXWWWWWWWWWWNNN
WWWWWWWN0xoc,',''.....'''.,kWWWWWWWWWWWWNN
WWWWWWWKl,''''''''''....','.'xNWWWWWWWWWWWN
WWWWWWNO:'''''''',''...''''''lXWWWWWWWWWWW
WWWWWWWk;,youpromise'.''''''',oXWWWWWWWWWW
WWWWWWWO:',,,''',,,,,',,,''''',c0WWWWWWWWW
WWWWWWNx;,;,,,,,,,,,,,,,,,,,;,,,:OWWWWWWWWW
WWWWWWXl,;,;,,,,,,,,,,,,,,,,,,,';OWWWWWWWWW
WWWWWWNOoc:;;;;,,,,,,,,,,,,,',;;cOWWWWWWWWW
WWWWWWWWNK0xlc:;;;;;;;;;;:okO0KNWWWWWWWWWW
WWWWWWWWWWWWWXKK0ko:;:cclx0NWWWWWWWWWWWWWWW
WWWWWWWWWWWWWWWWWNOlxKXNWWWWWWWWWWWWWWWWWWW
WWWWWWWWWWWWWWWWWWKdOWWWWWWWWWWWWWWWWWWWWWW
WNNNNWWWWWWWWWWWWWXdkWWWWWWWWWWWWWWWWWWWWWW
xdoodxOXWWWWWWWWWWNxkNWWWWWWWWWWWWWWWWWWWWW
l,,;;::lxO0NWWWWWWNxkNWWWWWWWWWWWWWWWWWWWWW
Xkc,;:::::cxXWWWWWNxkNWWWWWWWWWWWWWWWWWWWWN
WWXx:;::clod0WWWWWNxkNNWWWWWWNNNNWWWWWWWWNN
WWWWKkxxkOKXNWWWWWNxxXNWWNklc::cokKNWWNNNNN
WWWWWWWNWWWWWWWWWWWkxXNNOxc,''...',:xKNNNNN
NWWWWWWWWWWWWWWWWWWxxNN0:,;;,'..''.'dXNNNNN
NNNNWWWWWWWWWWWWWWWNxkNNO:,,,,,''...:0NXXXXX
NNNNNNNNWWWWWWWWWWWXdkNWNd;;;,;;;,',xXXXXXXX
XNNNNNNNNNNNNNNNNNWKodKXNk::;,;:c:;c0NXXXXXX
```

```
WWWWWWWWWWWWWWWWWWWWWWWWWWWWWWWWWWWWWWWWNNN
WWWWWWWWWWWWWWWWWWWWWWWWWWWWWWWWWWWWWWWWWWN
WWWWWWWWWWWWWWWWWWWWWWWWWWWWWWWWWWWWWWWWWWW
WWWWWWWWWWWWWWWWWWWWWWWWWWWWWWWWWWWWWWWWWWW
WWWWWWWWWWWWWWWWWWWWWWWWWWWWWWWWWWWWWWWWWWW
WWWWWWWWWWWWWWNWWWWWWWWWWWWWWWWWWWWWWWWWWWW
WWWWWWWWWWWWN0xkXWWWKOxdO0KNWWWWWWWWWWWWWWW
WWWWWWWWWWNKxc;:lool:;,,,;;dNWWWWWWWWWWWWWW
WWWWWWWWKxoc;;;;,,,,''',;;,c0WWWWWWWWWWWWWW
WWWWWWWNkc;;;;;;;;;,'',,,;;;kWWWWWWWWWWWWWW
WWWWWWWXd:;:::;;;;;;;;;,;;;;l0WWWWWWWWWWWWW
WWWWWWWNx:::::;::::::::::;;,;cONWWWWWWWWWWW
WWWWWWWNxcc::cccc::cccccccc:c:dNWWWWWWWWWWW
WWWWWWWKdccccloolcclllccc::::;oXWWWWWWWWWWW
WWWWWWWNOooolllllclllcccc::cloxXWWWWWWWWWWW
WWWWWWWWWXK0kxdllllllllclx0KNNWWWWWWWWWWWWW
WWWWWWWWWWWWWNXKOkolodxkKNWWWWWWWWWWWWWWWWW
WWWWWWWWWWWWWWWWWW0kKNNWWWWWWWWWWWWWWWWWWWW
WWWWWWWWWWWWWWWWWWKkKWWWWWWWWWWWWWWWWWWWWWW
WWWWWWWWWWWWWWWWWWXkKMWWWWWWWWWWWWWWWWWWWWW
WWWWWWWWWWWWWWWWWMXk0MWWWWWWWWWWWWWWWWWWWWW
WWWWWWWWWWWWWWWWWMNk0WWWWWWWWWWWWWWWWWWWWWW
WWWWWWWWWWWWWWWWWMNO0WWWWWNNXXNWWWWWWWWWWWW
WWWWWWWWWWWWWWWWWWWOOWWWW0dlc:cox0XWWWWWWWW
WWWWWWWWWWWWWWWWWWWOOWWKxoc:;,,,,,l0WWWWWWW
WWWWWWWWWWWWWWWWWWNOOWNk::::;,,'',dNWWWWWWW
WWWWWWWWWWWWWWWWWMNkOWW0l;;;;:;,'cKWWWWWWWW
WWWWWWWWWWWWWWWWWMNxOWWNd::;,:l:,dNWWWWWWWW
```

```
XXXXXXNNNNNNNNNNNNNNNNNNNNNNNNNNNXXXXXXXXXX
XNNNNNNNNNNNNNNNWWWNNNNNNNNNNNNNNNNNNXXXXXX
NNNNNNNNNWWWWWWWWWWWWWWWWWNNNNNNNNNNNNNXXXX
NNNNNWWWNWWWWWWWWWWWWWWWWWWWWNNNNNNNNNNNNXX
NNNWWWWWWWWWWWWNOxXWWWWWN0OKXNWWWWWWNNNNNNN
WWWWWWWWWWWWNX0o;,cdkkxdc,';;:o0NWWWWNNNNNN
WWWWWWWWWW0xdl;''''.......'''..lXWWWWWWWNNN
WWWWWWWWWXo,'''''..'',''....'...cKWWWWWWWNNN
WWWWWWWWW0c'''''''',''......''.;ONWWWWWWWWN
WWWWWWWWW0:''''''''''''''''''''':ONWWWWWWWW
WWWWWWWWWKl',,,''',,''',,,,'''''';kNWWWWWWW
WWWWWWWWWO:,,,,,,,,,,,,,,,,,,,,,,'dNWWWWWWW
WWWWWWWWNd;,,,,,,,,,,,,,,,,,''''''lXWWWWWWW
WWWWWWWWW0o:::;;;,,,,,,,,,,''''';;dXWWWWWWW
WWWWWWWWWWNX0koc:;,,,;,,,;,;cdk00XNWWWWWWWW
WWWWWWWWWWWWWWNK0Oxl:;;;;cokXWWWWWWWWWWWWWW
WWWWWWWWWWWWWWWWWWWN0xlo0XNWWWWWWWWWWWWWWWW
WWWXOk0XXXXXNWWWWWWWWNKdxWWWWWWWWWWWWWWWWWW
WWWN0dIAMKEYodOKNWWWWNXxxNMWWMWWWWWWWWWWWWW
WWWWWNKko:;;,,;:d0NWWXxdNWWWWWWWWWWWWWWWWWN
WWWWWWWWX0dc;;;,,;dXWNxdNWWWWWWWWWWWWWWWWWN
WWWWWWWWWWNKkoc::;;dXWkdXWWWWWWWWWWWWWWWNNN
WWWWWWWWWWWWWNXK0Ok0NWkdXWWWWWNNNNNWWWNNNNN
WWWWWWWWWWWWWWWWWWWWWWkdXWWWOolcccox0NNNNNN
NNWWWWWWWWWWWWWWWWWWWWkdXN0kl,,'''.',:o0NNN
NNNNWWWWWWWWWWWWWWWWWWkdXKl,;;,'.'''..:0NXX
NNNNNNNWWWWWWWWWWWWWNNxdN0c,,,,,'....,kXXXX
NNNNNNNNNNNNNNNWWNWWNXxdNNx;;,,;;;''oKXXXXX
XXXXXXXNNNNNNNNNNNNNX0ooKNOc;;;,;cc;;kXXXXX
```

```
WWWWWWWWWWWWWWWWWWWWWWWWWWWWWWWWWWWWWWWWWWW
WWWWWWWWWWWWWWWWWWWWWWWWWWWWWWWWWWWWWWWWWWW
WWWWWWWWWWWWWWWWWWWWWWWWWWWWWWWWWWWWWWWWWWW
WWWWWWWWWWWWWWWWWWWWWWWWWWWWWWWWWWWWWWWWWWW
WWWWWWWWWWWWWWWWWWWWWWWWWWWWWWWWWWWWWWWWWWW
WWWWWWWWWWWWWNWWWWWWWWWWWWWWWWWWWWWWWWWWWWW
WWWWWWWWWWWXOx0NWWNOdodxxOXWWWWWWWWWWWWWWWW
WWWWWWWNX0kl:,,coc:;''''',lKWWWWWWWWWWWWWWW
WWWWWWXxc;;;;,''''..''.',,:ONWWWWWWWWWWWWWW
WWWWWW0c;;;;,,'',,.......';kNNWWWWWWWWWWWWW
WWWWWWk;,,',,;;,,'..''''',,cONNWWWWWWWWWWWW
WWWWWW0c,;:;',,;:;,;;;,',,,,:xXWNWWWWWWWWWW
WWWWWW0l;::;,,;,;;;::;;,,;,,':ONWWWWWWWWWWW
WWWWWW0l:::::c:;;;;,,',;;;,,,oXWWWWWWWWWWWW
WWWWWW0dc:cc::c;,,,''''''''';ckNWWWWWWWWWWW
WWWWWWWN0dccc:;,,;,,,''....l0XNWWWWWWWWWWWW
WWWWWWWWWN0xo:,:ccc;,'''';dXWNWWWWWWWWWWWWW
WWWWWWWWWWWWNKkkkodkxkOOXNWWWWWWWWWWWWWWWWW
WWWWWWWWWWWWWWWWWNkOWNNWWWWWWWWWWWWWWWWWWWW
WWWWWWWWWWWWWWWWWWOONWWWWWWWWWWWWWWWWWWWWWW
WWWWWWWWWWWWWWWWWWOkNWWWWWWWWWWWWWWWWWWWWWW
WWWWWWWWWWWWWWWWWW0kNWWWWWWWWWWWWWWWWWWWWWW
WWWWWWWWWWWWWWWWWW0kXWWWWWWWWWWWWWWWWWWWWWW
WWWWWWWWWWWWWWWWWWKkXWWWX00kxk0NWWWWWWWWWWW
WWWWWWWWWWWWWWWWWWKxKWNKOl:,',:ok0KNWWWWWWW
WWWWWWWWWWWWWWWWWM0dOXkc:lc,,,,;:ckXNWWWWWW
WWWWWWWWWWWWWWWWWW0x0NOc;lxl;;,,,lKWWWWWWWW
WWWWWWWWWWWWWWWWWWOdXWNkok0kocc;:kNNWWWWWWW
WWWWWWWWWWWWWWWWWWklOXNKO00OxddclkKXNWWWWWW
```

```
XXXXXNNNNNNNNNNNNNNNNNNNNNNNNNNNNNXXXXXXXXX

XXXNNNNNNNNNNNNNNNNNNNNNNNNNNNNNNNNNNXXXXXX
NNNNNNNNNNNWWWWWWWWWWWWWWWWWNNNNNNNNNNNNXXX
NNNNNNWWNNNWWWWWWWNNWWWWWWWWWWWNNWWNNNNNNNNNXX
NNNNWWWWWWWWWWWNKddKNWWWWWKxxO0KNWWWWWNNNNNNNN
NNNWWWWWWWWWNX0d:,,:odool;..,,,l0WWWWWNNNNNN
WWWWWWWWWXOoc;'''''.......'''.'dNWWWWWWNNNN
WWWWWWWWWKl''''''..'''.....'...oNWWWWWWNNNN
WWWWWWWWNk;'''''''''''......''';OWWWWWWNNNN
WWWWWWWWWk:'''''''D-Y,,'''''''.':ONWWWWWWNN
WWWWWWWWWO:'',,''',,,,,,,,,''''';kWWWWWWN
WWWWWWWWNx;,,,,,,,,,,,,,,,,,,,,,',kWWWWWWN
WWWWWWWWXo,,,,,,,,,,,,,,,,,'''''''dNWWWWWWN
WWWWWWWWWKdlc:;;;,,,,,,,,,,,'';::lONWWWWWWN
WWWWWWWWWWWNNXOdlc:;,,,,,,,;:dOKXNNWWWWWWNWN
WWWWWWWWWWWWWWNXK0kdc:;:clxKNWWWWWWWWWWWWWN
WWWWWWWWWWWWWWWWWWWW0dlxXNWWWMWWWWWWWWWWWNN
WWWWWWWWWWWWWWWWWWWWKkokWWWWWWWWWWWWWWWWWWNN
WWWWWWWWWWWWWWWWWWWWXOokWWWWXOxkKNWWWWWWWNN
WWWWWWWWWWWWWWWWWWWWX0dxWWWXx:;;lkKNNNWWNNN
WWWWWWWWWWWWWWWWWWWWNKdxWN0o;,,,,:lxO0KXXXN
WWWWWWWWWWWWWWWWWWWWNKdxN0l,''.'',,;;:cllxX
WWWWWWWWWWWWWWWWWWWWNXxxNXOxl;'.''''''..,oX
NNWWWWWWWWWWWWWWWWWWNXxxNWWXd;''''.''..'cON
NNNNWWWWWWWWWWWWWWWWNXxxNXko:,'''.....,lkKX
NNNNNNNNWWWWWWWWWWWWNKdxNk;',;,.......oKXXX
NNNNNNNNNNNNNNNNWWNWX0dxNO:',,,,'....:0XXXX
XXXXXNNNNNNNNNNNNNWKkoxNXd;;,,,;;,',xKXXXX
XXXXXXXXXXXXNNNNNNN0dcdXXx:;;,,;::,c0XKXXX
```

```
WWWWWWWWWWWWWWWWWWWWWWWWWWWWWWWWWWWWWWWWWWW
WWWWWWWWWWWWWWWWWWWWWWWWWWWWWWWWWWWWWWWWWWW
WWWWWWWWWWWWWWWWWWWWWWWWWWWWWWWWWWWWWWWWWWW
WWWWWWWWWWWWWWWXKWWWWWWWNWWWWWWWWWWWWWWWWWW
WWWWWWWWWWWWNXklcdKXKKKxlodxONWWWWWWWWWWWWW
WWWWWWWWWXOxoc;,'';:;,'',''',dXWWWWWWWWWWWW
WWWWWWWWWx;;;;;,''''...''.',,lKWWWWWWWWWWWW
WWWWWWWWKl,,,,,,IDONTWANTTO''c0NNNWWWWWWWWW
WWWWWWWWKl;;,,,,,;;,'....'''',oKNNNWWWWWWWW
WWWWWWWWNd;:::;;;;c:,,,,,''',,,l0NNNWWWWWWW
WWWWWWWWXd:::;::;;:;;,;;;,,,;,';kNNNWWWWWWW
WWWWWWWW0l::c:cccc;;;;;;;;,,;;,;kWWWWWWWWWW
WWWWWWWWXkdlllc:;;,,,;;;,,''''':OWWWWWWWWWW
WWWWWWWWWWNKOxo:;,;::::;;clodxk0NWWWWWWWWWW
WWWWWWWWWWWWWNXKKOxlclodk0NNNNWWWWWWWWWWWWW
WWWWWWWWWWWWWWWWWWW0xkKNWWWWWWWWWWWWWWWWWWW
WWWWWWWWWWWWWWWWWWWKkkKWWWWWWWWWWWWWWWWWWWW
WWWWWWWWWWWWWWWWWWWKkkKWWWWWWWWWWWWWWWWWWWW
WWWWWWWWWWWWWWWWWWMKkkKWWWWWWWWWWWWWWWWWWWW
WWWWWWWWWWWWWWWWWWMKkkKWWWWWWWWWWWWWWWWWWWW
WWWWWWWWWWWWWWWWWWMXkkKWWWWWWWWWWWWWWWWWWWW
WWWWWWWWWWWWWWWWWWWXkkKWWNX0OOkKNWMWWWWWWWW
WWWWWWWWWWWWWWWWWWWKxx0NXOo:;,,:ok0XWWWWWWW
WWWWWWWWWWWWWWWWWWWKdokOc:cc,,,,;:lOXNWWWWW
WWWWWWWWWWWWWWWWWWW0xk0k:,coc;,,,,dXNNWWWWW
WWWWWWWWWWWX0OOOOKNkd0XXxldkxlcc;c0NWWWWWWW
WWWWWWWWWWKoccccccoxlcx0000Okddocd0KXWWWWWW
```

```
WWWWWWWWWWWWWWWWWWWWWWWWWWWWWWWWWWWWNNNNN
WWWWWWWWWWWWWWWWWWWWWWWWWWWWWWWWWWWWWWWWW
WWWWWWWWWWWWWWWWWWWWWWWWWWWWWWWWWWWWWWWWW
WWWWWWWWWWWWWWWWWWWWWWWWWWWWWWWWWWWWWWWWW
WWWWWWWWWWWWWWWWWWWWWWWWWWWWWWWWWWWWWWWWW
WWWWWWWWWWWWNKxkXNWWNXkkO0KNWWWWWWWWWWWWW
WWWWWWWWWWX0Odc,,:loc::,''';dKWWWWWWWWWWW
WWWWWWWWW0c:;,;,'''....'..,,:ONWWWWWWWWWW
WWWWWWWWWXd;;;;,,'','''....'',xXNNNWWWWWWWWW
WWWWWWWWWKl,;,,,,;;,,'....'''':OXNNNWWWWWWWW
WWWWWWWWWNd;::;,;;:c:,,,,,''''';dKNNNWWWWWWW
WWWWWWWWWXd;:c:;;:;;:;,;;,,,,,;,'cKNNNWWWWWWW
WWWWWWWWW0l::ccccc:;,;;;;,,,,,,'c0WNWWWWWWWW
WWWWWWWWWXkdlclc:;,,,,,,;;,'''',;oKWNWWWWWWWW
WWWWWWWWWWWNK0xoc;;;;;::;:ldxk0KXNNNNWWWWWWW
WWWWWWWWWWWWWWNXXX0kolloxOXNNNNNNWWWWWWWWWWW
WWWWWWWWWWWWWWWWWWW0xkKNWWWWWWWWWWWWWWWWWWW
WWWWWWWWWWWWWWWWWWMKxkKWWWWWWWWWWWWWWWWWWW
WWWWWWWWWWWWWWWWWWWWKxx0WWWWWWWWWWWWWWWWWWW
WWWWWWWWWWWWWWWWWWWWXxdOWWWWWWWWWWWWWWWWWWW
WWWWWWWWWWWWWWWWWWWWXkoOWWWWWWWWWWWWWWWWWWW
WWWWWWWWWWWWWWWWWWWWNkoOWWWWWWWWWWWWWWWWWWW
WWWWWWWWWWWWWWWWWWWWNkoONWWX0OkxkKNWWWWWWWW
WWWWWWWWWWWWWWWWWWWWNklkNXKx:;,',:oxOKNWWWWW
WWWWWWWWWWWWWWWWWWWWNd:o0d:cc;''',;:lkXXNWWW
WWWWWWWWWWWWWWWWWWWWXxlxOl,;ll;,,'',oKNNWWWW
WWWWWWWWWWWWWNNXXXNWKdlONkccoxoc::,:kXWWWWWW
WWWWWWWWWWW0xddookXOc:xNKxk0OxolL:lOKXNWWWW
```

```
WWWWWWWWWWWWWWWWWWWWWWWWWWWWWWWWWWWWWWWNNNN
WWWWWWWWWWWWWWWWWWWWWWWWWWWWWWWWWWWWWWWWWWN
WWWWWWWWWWWWWWWWWWWWWWWWWWWWWWWWWWWWWWWWWWW
WWWWWWWWWWWWXKNWWWWWWWWWWWWWWWWWWWWWWWWWWWW
WWWWWWWWWWWNd:oOXNWWWWWWNXNNWWWWWWWWWWWWWWW
WWWWWWWWWWXd;,,,:oxkkkxdl:clkXNWWWWWWWWWWWW
WWWWWWWXOxl;,,'''''''',,,,,,;dNWWWWWWWWWWWW
WWWWWWNkcc:,,,,,',cl:;,'',;,,xWWWWWWWWWWWWW
WWWWWWWOl;;;;;;;,:olc:,',;;,,cKWWWWWWWWWWWW
WWWWWWNk:;:;;IAMSORRY;;,;,,;;dXWWWWWWWWWWWW
WWWWWWWOc::;:::::::::;;::;;;:OWWWWWWWWWWWWW
WWWWWWWN0dc:::::ccc::::cc:;,:0WWWWWWWWWWWWW
WWWWWWWWWXxc::cloolcllllc:::xNWWWWWWWWWWWWW
WWWWWWWWWWKdllllloollllcc:;cOWWWWWWWWWWWWWW
WWWWWWWWWWWKxdoollcoolccx00KNWWWWWWWWWWWWWW
WWWWWWWWWWWWNKOOkkdkXX00XWWWWWWWWWWWWWWWWWW
WWWWWWWWWWWWWWWWWWkkNMMWWWWWWWWWWWWWWWWWWWW
WWWWWWWWWWWWWWWWWWOxNMWWWWWWWWWWWWWWWWWWWWW
WWWWWWWWWWWWWWWWWW0xXMWWWWWWWWWWWWWWWWWWWWW
WWWWWWWWWWWWWWWWWM0xKMWWWWWWWWWWWWWWWWWWWWW
WWWWWWWWWWWWWWWWWMKxKMMWWWWWWWWWWWWWWWWWWWW
WWWWWWWWWWWWWWWWWWKxKMWWWWWNXKKXNWWWWWWWWWW
WWWWWWWWWWWWWWWWWWKd0MMWNKo::;;cdONWWWWWWWW
WWWWWWWWWWWWWWWWWWKd0MWKdl:,''''.';oXWWWWWW
WWWWWWWWWWWWWWWWWW0oOWNd,,,,''....,xNWWWWWW
WWWWWNXKkkOK0kdoll:,:ll:'''''''..'xWWWWWWWW
WWWWXko:'.',,'..',,,''''.'''.','.;0WWWWWWWW
```

```
XNNNNNNWWWWWWWWWWWWWWWWWWWWWWWWWWNNNNNXXX
NNNWWWWWWWWWWWWWWWWWWWWWWWWWWWWWWWWWNNNNX
WWWWWWWWWWWWWWWWWWWWWWWWWWWWWWWWWWWWWWWNNN
WWWWWWWWWWWWWWWWWWWWWWWWWWWWWWWWWWWWWWWWWW
WWWWWWWWWWWWWWWWWWWWWWWWWWWWWWWWWWWWWWWWWW
WWWWWWWWWWWNKKWWWWWWWWN0OXWWWWWWWWWWWWWWWW
WWWWWWWWWWNk:ckXNXKOdol;,oO0KNWWWWWWWWWWWW
WWWWWWWWXOx:,,,:l:,,'''',;,,c0WWWWWWWWWWWW
WWWWWWWXo;,,,,,,,'',''''',,,,;xWWWWWWWWWWW
WWWWWWWO:,,,;;,,;,,,,,,,,,;,:0WWWWWWWWWWWW
WWWWWWWO:,;,;;;;:cc:;;;;;;::,cKWWWWWWWWWWW
WWWWWWWKo:;;:::::cccccc:;;;;:OWWWWWWWWWWWW
WWWWWWWKo:ccccc::llcclc::c:;:xNWWWWWWWWWWW
WWWWWWW0l:cclllllllllccccccxXWWWWWWWWWWWWW
WWWWWWWW0dollc::cccccccc:::oOXNWWWWWWWWWWW
WWWWWWWWWNKkkocdddddxkxddO0KWWWWWWWWWWWWWW
WWWWWWWWWWWWWWNNWWWOxKMWWWWWWWWWWWWWWWWWWW
WWWWWWWWWWWWWWWWWWW0xKMWWWWWWWWWWWWWWWWWWW
WWWWWWWWWWWWWWWWWWMKxKMWWWWWWWWWWWWWWWWWWW
WWWWWWWWWWWWWWWWWWMKx0MWWWWWWWWWWWWWWWWWWW
WWWWWWWWWWWWWWWWWWWKx0MMWWWWWWWWWWWWWWWWWW
WWWWWWWWWWWWWWWWWWWXx0MMWWWWWWWWWWWWWWWWWW
WWWWWWWWWWWWWWWWWWWXx0MWWWWWWWWWWWWWWWWWWW
WWWWWWWWWWWWWWWWWWMXxOMWWWXkddddkXWWWWWWWW
WWWWWWWWWWWWWWWWWWWXxOMWX0d;''..';lx0NWWWW
WWWWWWWWWWWWWWWWWWWKdOMNd,,,,'......lXWWWW
WWWWWWWWWWXXWWWWXxoc;cxd;.''''.....:KWWWWW
WWWNKkdol:cox0Kl.....''...'..''..'kWWWWWWW
NWW0l;;,..',,od;...''''......'',.:KWWWWWWW
```

```
WWWWWWWWWWWWWWWWWWWWWWWWWWWWWWWWWWWWWWWWWWW
WWWWWWWWWWWWWWWWWWWWWWWWWWWWWWWWWWWWWWWWWWW
WWWWWWWWWWWWWWWWWWWWWWWWWWWWWWWWWWWWWWWWWWW
WWWWWWWWWWWWWWWWWWWWWWWWWWWWWWWWWWWWWWWWWWW
WWWWWWWWWWWWWWWWWWWWWWWWWWWWWWWWWWWWWWWWWWW
WWWWWWWWWWWWWWKkKNWWWWWWNXNWWWWWWWWWWWWWWWW
WWWWWWWWWWWWNOocldk0kkkxdlldkKNWWWWWWWWWWWW
WWWWWWWWWWN0xc;::;;,,,,;;;;;;dXWWWWWWWWWWWW
WWWWWWWWWXxlc;;;;::lolc;,;::;lKWWWWWWWWWWWW
WWWWWWWWWXxc::::::lolc:;;;::;c0WWWWWWWWWWWW
WWWWWWWWWNxcc::ccc:::c::;::::dNWWWWWWWWWWWW
WWWWWWWWWNkc:cc:::ccc:::cc::;dNWWWWWWWWWWWW
WWWWWWWWWWN0dccccclcccccccccckWWWWWWWWWWWWW
WWWWWWWWWWWWKoccllollllllc::l0WWWWWWWWWWWWW
WWWWWWWWWWWWNOdollllloolclxOKNWWWWWWWWWWWWW
WWWWWWWWWWWWWNK0kxxdxKXKOKNWWWWWWWWWWWWWWWW
WWWWWWWWWWWWWWWWNWWOkKNWWWWWWWWWWWWWWWWWWWW
WWWWWWWWWWWWWWWWWWW0k0XWWWWWWWWWWWWWWWWWWWW
WWWWWWWWWWWWWWWWWWW0kOXWWWWWWWWWWWWWWWWWWWW
WWWWWWWWWWWWWWWWWWWKkkKWWWWWWWWWWWWWWWWWWWW
WWWWWWWWWWWWWWWWWWWKxkKMWWWWWWWWWWWWWWWWWWW
WWWWWWWWWWWWWWWWWWWKkkKWWWWNXXKXNWWWWWWWWWW
WWWWWWWWWWWWWWWWWWMKxkKWWWXdc:;;cokXWWWWWWW
WWWWWWWWWWWWWWWWWWWKxxKWXxlc;,,,''';xXWWWWW
WWWWWWWWWWWWWWWNKXXklcooc;',;,,'''':0WWWWWW
WWMWNXKKXNNWWNkc:::;,,,'','..',,'.,kWWWWWWW
WWNOdoccldxx0Ko',,''''''',''...,;;'cKWWWWWWW
```

```
NNNNNNNNNNNNNNNNNNNNNNNNNNNNNNNNNNNXXXXX
NNNNNNWWWWWWWWWWWWWWWWWWWWNNNNNNNNNNNNNX
NNWWWWWWWWWWWWWWWWWWWWWWWWWWWWNNNNNNNNNN
WWWWWWWWWWWWWWWWWWWWWWWWWWWWWWWWWNNNNNNN
WWWWWWWWWWWWWWWWWWWWWWWWWWWWWWWWWWNNNNNN
WWWWWWWWWWWWWKOKWWWWWWWWWNNXNWWWWWWWWWWWWWWWNNN
WWWWWWWWWWWN0l;:oxkxxddlc:cdKWWWWWWWWWWWWWNN
WWWWWWWWWWN0d:,,,'...''''''''dNWWWWWWWWWWWWWW
WWWWWWWWWNx:;,''',;:;,'.',,'lKWWWWWWWWWWWWWW
WWWWWWWWWWk:,,'',',;;,'''','':OWWWWWWWWWWWWWW
WWWWWWWWWNd,,,,,;,,,,''''''',dNWWWWWWWWWWWWWW
WWWWWWWWWNk:,,,,,,,,,,,,,,,''oNWWWWWWWWWWWWWW
WWWWWWWWWWNXkc,,;;;;,;;;;;;,;xWWWWWWWWWWWWWW
WWWWWWWWWWWWNx:;;;;;;;;;;;;;lOWWWWWWWWWWWWWW
WWWWWWWWWWWWW0l;::::cloc;lOKXNWWWWWWWWWWWWWWW
WWWWWWWWWWN0xc:;cxxodKWXOKWWWWWWWWWWWWWWWWWWW
WWWWWWWWWNkc;::lONM0xKMWWWWWWWWWWWWWWWWWWWWW
WWWWWWWWNx::::lOWWMKx0MMWWWWWWWWWWWWWWWWWWWWWW
WWWWWWWOc:cclOWWWWXx0WWWWWWWWWWWWWWWWWWWWWWWW
WWWWWWXdcc:ckNWWWWXxOWWWWWWWWWWWWWWWWWWWWWWWW
WWWWWWXkddoONWWWWWNxOMWWWWWWWWWMWWWWWWWWWWWW
WWWWWWWNXXNWWNNNNNXxOWWWWWNKK00KNWWWWWWWWWW
WWWWWWWWWWWXkllodllcxXNWNKd:;;,;lxOKNWWWNWW
WWWWWWWWWWNx;,,'',,,cd0Nxc:;,''''',dXWWNNNN
WWWWWWWWWWXkc;,,'',,:lO0:,,;,''''':0WNNNNNN
WWWWWWWWWWNKKOl;,,'',;ckKl,,;;;;,',xNWNNNNNN
WNWWWNKOOxcldo;;,,'';cONx:;;;;::;c0WNNNNNNN
```

```
WWWWWWWWWWWWWWWWWWWWWWWWWWWWWWWWWWWWWWWWWNN
WWWWWWWWWWWWWWWWWWWWWWWWWWWWWWWWWWWWWWWWWWW
WWWWWWWWWWWWWWWWWWWWWWWWWWWWWWWWWWWWWWWWWWW
WWWWWWWWWWWWWWWWWWWWWWWWWWWWWWWWWWWWWWWWWWW
WWWWWWWWWWWWWWWWWWWWWWWWWWWWWWWWWWWWWWWWWWW
WWWWWWWWWWWWNWWWWWWWWWWWWWWWWWWWWWWWWWWWWWW
WWWWWWWWWWWW0x0XNWWKOOOkxdkNWWWWWWWWWWWWWWW
WWWWWWWWWWW01:cldxxl;;;:;,:dKNWWWWWWWWWWWWW
WWWWWWWWWWKd:;;;,,,,,,;;,,,;:kWWWWWWWWWWWWW
WWWWWWWWN0dlc:;,,;cl:;;,;:;,;kWWWWWWWWWWWWW
WWWWWWWWKdllc::;;cooc;;;;:;,c0WWWWWWWWWWWWW
WWWWWWWWKocc::::;;;;;;;;;;;;c0WWWWWWWWWWWWW
WWWWWWWWNkl:::;;;::c:;;;::;,c0WWWWWWWWWWWWW
WWWWWWWWWN0dl:::clllc::cccc:dXWWWWWWWWWWWWW
WWWWWWWWWWWKdccllloolccclc:ckNWWWWWWWWWWWWW
WWWWWWWWWWWNOoooollllllccok0NWWWWWWWWWWWWWW
WWWWWWWWWWWWN0kddollloloOXWWWMWWWWWWWWWWWWW
WWWWWWWWWWWWWWNXKXkx0XXNWWWWWWWWWWWWWWWWWWW
WWWWWWWWWWWWWWWWWW0xXMWWWWWWWWWWWWWWWWWWWWW
WWWWWWWWWWWWWWWWWWKxKMWWWWWWWWWWWWWWWWWWWWW
WWWWWWWWWWWWWWWWWWKkKMWWWWWWWWWWWWWWWWWWWWW
WWWWWWWWWWWWWWWWWWKkKMWWWWWWWWWWWWWWWWWWWWW
WWWWWWWWWWWWWWWWWWXk0MWWWWWWWKOOkOKXWWWWWWW
WWWWWWWWWWWWWWWWWWXk0MMWWWWXOo;;,',cd0XNWWW
WWWWWWWWWWWWWWWWWWXk0WWWWW01;::,''''',oKWWW
WWWWWWWWWWWWWNWNK0kldOOOK0c,,,;,'''.'l0WWWW
WWWWWWWWWNNKkodo:;,,,,,;c:'',,,,,'..lXWWWWW
```

```
WWWWWWWWWWWWWWWWWWWWWWWWWWWWWWWWWWWWWWWWWWWWWW
WWWWWWWWWWWWWWWWWWWWWWWWWWWWWWWWWWWWWWWWWWWWWW
WWWWWWWWWWWWWWWWWWWWWWWWWWWWWWWWWWWWWWWWWWWWWW
WWWWWWWWWWWWWWWWWWWWWWWWWWWWWWWWWWWWWWWWWWWWWW
WWWWWWWWWWWWWWWWWWWWWWWWWWWWWWWWWWWWWWWWWWWWWW
WWWWWWWWWWXXNWWWWWWNNNNXXWWWWWWWWWWWWWWWWWWWWW
WWWWWWWWWNKdlxOXNXOdooolclOWWWWWWWWWWWWWWWWWWW
WWWWWWWWWXx::;:cll:;::;;;;:x0NWWWWWWWWWWWWWWWW
WWWWWWWWXkl:;;,,,',;;,,,;,,,lKWWWWWWWWWWWWWWWW
WWWWWWNOollc:;;,;loc;',;:;,,lXWWWWWWWWWWWWWWWW
WWWWWWXxllcc::;;:ll:;;;;;,,;dWWWWWWWWWWWWWWWWW
WWWWWWNxccc::;:;;;;;;,,;;;;;oXWWWWWWWWWWWWWWWW
WWWWWWN0dc:::;;;::c:;;;::;;:kNWWWWWWWWWWWWWWWW
WWWWWWWWXklc:;:ccllc::ccc;lKWWWWWWWWWWWWWWWWWW
WWWWWWWWWNOlcclloolccccc::dXWWWWWWWWWWWWWWWWWW
WWWWWWWWWWXxllllllllccclx0NWWWWWWWWWWWWWWWWWWW
WWWWWWWWWWWXOxdolcclllokXWWWWWWWWWWWWWWWWWWWWW
WWWWWWWWWWWWWNKKKxdKXNNWWWWWWWWWWWWWWWWWWWWWWW
WWWWWWWWWWWWWWWWWkxNMWWWWWWWWWWWWWWWWWWWWWWWWW
WWWWWWWWWWWWWWWWWOxXWWWWWWWWWWWWWWWWWWWWWWWWWW
WWWWWWWWWWWWWWWWWOxXWWWWWWWWWWWWWWWWWWWWWWWWWW
WWWWWWWWWWWWWWWWW0dKWWWWWWWWWWWMWWWWWWWWWWWWWW
WWWWWWWWWWWWWWWWM0d0WWWWWWWWXK0OO0XWWWWWWWWWWW
WWWWWWWWWWWWWWWWKd0WWWWWWWKo;,'.',cdOKNWWWWW
WWWWWWWWWWWWWWWXKklxXXNWWkc:,'......'oXWWWWW
WWWWWWWWWWWWWNKd:;;,;ccldo;.'''......cKWWWWWW
WWWWWWWWWNNNWXx:,,,;;;;;;;'.....'....;0WWWWWW
WWWNK0OOdxOo,,;,,:::::;;,......'''.:XMWWWWWW
```

```
WWWWWWWWWWWWWWWWWWWWWWWWWWWWWWWWWWWWWWWWWWW
WWWWWWWWWWWWWWWWWWWWWWWWWWWWWWWWWWWWWWWWWWW
WWWWWWWWWWWWWWWWWWWWWWWWWWWWWWWWWWWWWWWWWWW
WWWWWWWWWWWWWWWWWWWWWWWWWWWWWWWWWWWWWWWWWWW
WWWWWWWWWWWWWWWWWWWWWWWWWWWWWWWWWWWWWWWWWWW
WWWWWWWWWWWWWWWWWWWWWWWWWWWWWWWWWWWWWWWWWWW
WWWWWWWWWWWWWWKxd0NWXX0OXNWWWWWWWWWWWWWWWWW
WWWWWWWWWWWWWN0l;:cdko:::cood0WWWWWWWWWWWWW
WWWWWWWWWWWNKxl:::;,;,,,;;;;;l0NWWWWWWWWWWWW
WWWWWWWWWNOolc:::;,;:c:;,,,;;cdXWWWWWWWWWWW
WWWWWWWWWN0l:;;;:cllool;;,,,;l0NWWWWWWWWWWW
WWWWWWWWWW0l::;;:::;::;;;;;;;cOWWWWWWWWWWWW
WWWWWWWWWWWNkoc::::::::;;:;:::kNWWWWWWWWWWW
WWWWWWWWWWWWX0l::cclc:::cccc:lKWWWWWWWWWWWW
WWWWWWWWWWWWWNXkdooolcccccccoONWWWWWWWWWWWW
WWWWWWWWWWWWWWWNXOxoodxxxxOKNWWWWWWWWWWWWWW
WWWWWWWWWWWWWWWWWWXxONNWWWWWWWWWWWWWWWWWWWW
WWWWWWWWWWWWWWWWWMNk0WWWWWWWWWWWWWWWWWWWWWW
WWWWWWWWWWWWWWWWWWXk0MWWWWWWWWWWWWWWWWWWWWW
WWWWWWWWWWWWWWWWWWXk0MWWWWWWWWWWWWWWWWWWWWW
WWWWWWWWWWWWWWWWWWXkKMWWWWWWWWWWWWWWWWWWWWW
WWWWWWWWWWWWWWWWWWXkKMWWWWWWWWWWWWWWWWWWWWW
WWWWWWWWWWWWWWWWWMKkXMWWWWWWWWXkdddxOXWWWWW
WWWWWWWWWWWWWWWWWKkXMWWWWWKxo:;,,',:d0XWWWW
WWWWWWWWWWWWNWNXXXkdKNNNW0l;;:;,,'''':OWWWW
WWWWNX000kxdlllc::;;cccoo:,,;,;,''''cONWWWW
WWWNOdlc:;;,''',,,,';;,'''.';,,;;,.cKWWWWWW
```

```
WWWWWWWWWWWWWWWWWWWWWWWWWWWWWWWWWWWWWWWWWWW
WWWWWWWWWWWWWWWWWWWWWWWWWWWWWWWWWWWWWWWWWWW
WWWWWWWWWWWWWWWWWWWWWWWWWWWWWWWWWWWWWWWWWWW
WWWWWWWWWWWWWWNNWWWWWWWWWWWWWWWWWWWWWWWWWWW
WWWWWWWWWWWWWXxd0NWWWWWWWWWWWWWWWWWWWWWWWWW
WWWWWWWWWWWWNk:;:coxxxkOXWWWWWWWWWWWWWWWWWW
WWWWWWWWWWWN0c;;,'',,,;:lxXWWWWWWWWWWWWWWWW
WWWWWWWWWWNOo::;,,;,',,;;;dXWWWWWWWWWWWWWWW
WWWWWWWWWXkllc:;;cdl;,,,,,:lkNWWWWWWWWWWWWW
WWWWWWWWWWNOoc;;;:ll:;,;,,,,;oKWWWWWWWWWWWWW
WWWWWWWWWWNOl:;;;;;;;,;:;;;:cxNWWWWWWWWWWWW
WWWWWWWWWWWXxc;:;;:c:;::::::;l0WWWWWWWWWWWW
WWWWWWWWWWWWX0xl::ccclcccccccoKWWWWWWWWWWWW
WWWWWWWWWWWWWWNXkoccllllcclllkXWWWWWWWWWWWW
WWWWWWWWWWMWWWWWXkoollodxxkOKNWWWWWWWWWWWWW
WWWWWWWWWWWWWWWWWNXKxlOWWWWWWWWWWWWWWWWWWWW
WWWWWWWWWWWWWWWWWWWNkoOWWWWWWWWWWWWWWWWWWWW
WWWWWWWWWWWWWWWWWWWNkoOWWWWWWWWWWWWWWWWWWWW
WWWWWWWWWWWWWWWWWWWNko0WWWWWWWWWWWWWWWWWWWW
WWWWWWWWWWWWWWWWWWWNko0WWWWWWWWWWWWWWWWWWWW
WWWWWWWWWWWWWWWWWWWXkd0WWWWWWWWWWWWWWWWWWWW
WWWWWWWWWWWWWWWWWWWXkxKWWWWWWWWX000KXWWWWWW
WWWWWWWWWWWWWWWWWWMKkkKWWWWNKOo::;;:oOXWWWW
WWWWWWWWWWWWNNNWWWM0xOXWWWNOl:c:,,,,',ckNWW
WWWWWWWWWNXOdodxOOOdoxk0KNOc,;;:,'''',l0WWW
WWWKOkkOOdl::cccc:;,;::cldc,,;,,;;,';xNWWWW
WWKo:cccc;,;:cccc:,';clollc;::,,;::'lXWWWWW
```

```
WWWWWWWWWWWWWWWWWWWWWWWWWWWWWWWWWWWWWWWNNNN
WWWWWWWWWWWWWWWWWWWWWWWWWWWWWWWWWWWWWWWWWWN
WWWWWWWWWWWWWWWWWWWWWWWWWWWWWWWWWWWWWWWWWWW
WWWWWWWWWWWWNkOXWWWWWWWWWWWWWWWWWWWWWWWWWWW
WWWWWWWWWWWWXl;:ox0K0OO0KNWWWWWWWWWWWWWWWWW
WWWWWWWWWWWWk:,''',;;;:::dXWWWWWWWWWWWWWWWW
WWWWWWWWWWWKo;,,,''',;::,:kXWWWWWWWWWWWWWWW
WWWWWWWWWWNkl:;,;;;,'',,,;;;lKWWWWWWWWWWWWWW
WWWWWWWWKxcc::;;:lddc;,,;:;l0WWWWWWWWWWWWWW
WWWWWWWWKdcc:;;;codko:;;;,:kWWWWWWWWWWWWWWW
WWWWWWWWWXkl:;;;;;::;;:;;,cONWWWWWWWWWWWWWW
WWWWWWWWWWNkl:;;;;;::;;;:cox0XNNNWWWWWWWWWWW
WWWWWWWWWWWNKOxlcll::clxKWX0XWWNNWWWWWWWWWWW
WWWWWWWWWWWWWWNXXX0ooOXNWWWWWWWWWWWWWWWWWWWW
WWWWWWWWWWWWWWWWWWW0xXMWWWWWWWWWWWWWWWWWWWWW
WWWWWWWWWWWWWWWWWWWKxKMWWWWWWWWWWWWWWWWWWWWW
WWWWWWWWWWWWWWWWWWMKxKMMWWWWWWWWWWWWWWWWWWWW
WWWWWWWWWWWWWWWWWWMKx0MWWWWWWWWWWWWWWWWWWWWW
WWWWWWWWWWWWWWWWWWMXx0MWWWWWWWWWWWWWWWWWWWWW
WWWWWWWWWWWWWWWWWWWXx0MMWWWWWWWWWWWWWWWWWWWW
WWWWWWWWWWWWWWWWWWWNkOMMWWWWWWWWNNNNWWWWWWWWW
WWWWWWWWWWWWWWWWWWWNxOWWWWWWWWNOolcclx0NWWWWW
WWWWWWWWWWWWWWWWWWWNxOWWWWWWWOlc;,'''',cxKWWW
WWWWWWWWWWWWWNNWWWWXxOWWWWWO:,,;,'..'.,l0WWW
WWWWWNKOkk0Oxddddo:lxxx00c',,',,'..;ONWWWW
WWWWKxc,,,;::;:::;;;,'',cc'.,,'',,'.oNWWWWW
```

```
NNNNNWWWWWWWWWWWWWWWWWWWWWWWWWWWWWWNNNNNXXXXK
NNWWWWWWWWWWWWWWWWWWWWWWWWWWWWWWWWWWWNNNNXXX
WWWWWWWWWWWWWWWWWWWWWWWWWWWWWWWWWWWWWWWNNNNX
WWWWWWWWWWWWWWWWWWWWWWWWWWWWWWWWWWWWWWWWWNNN
WWWWWWWWWWWWWWWWWWWWWWWWWWWWWWWWWWWWWWWWWWWN
WWWWWWWWWWWWWWNNWWWWWWWWWWWWWWWWWWWWWWWWWWWW
WWWWWWWWWWWWWNkok0XWWWWWWWWWWWWWWWWWWWWWWWWW
WWWWWWWWWWWWWKl,,,:oddoddkKWWWMWWWWWWWWWWWWW
WWWWWWWWWWWWNx:;,,,',;::;;dNWWWWWWWWWWWWWWWW
WWWWWWWWWWNKxc;;;;,,',,;;;:o0WWWWWWWWWWWWWWW
WWWWWWWWNOocc:;;;clc;,,;;;;dNWWWWWWWWWWWWWWW
WWWWWWWWXdlc:;;;cdkkc;;;;;lKWWWWWWWWWWWWWWWW
WWWWWWWWWXkl:;;;;;cc:;;;,,oXWWWWWWWWWWWWWWWW
WWWWWWWWWWNkc:;;;;;::;,;;cokXXXNWWWWWWWWWWWW
WWWWWWWWWWWNKOdcccc:::lkXN0KNNNWWWWWWWWWWWWW
WWWWWWWWWWWWWWNXKKkld0XWWWWWWWWWWWWWWWWWWWWW
WWWWWWWWWWWWWWWWWWXxOWWWWWWWWWWWWWWWWWWWWWWW
WWWWWWWWWWWWWWWWWWNxONWWWWWWWWWWWWWWWWWWWWWW
WWWWWWWWWWWWWWWWWWNkkNWWWWWWWWWWWWWWWWWWWWWW
WWWWWWWWWWWWWWWWWWWkkNWWWWWWWWWWWWWWWWWWWWWW
WWWWWWWWWWWWWWWWWWWkxNNWWWWWWWWWWWWWWWWWWWWW
WWWWWWWWWWWWWWWWWWWkxXNWWWWWWWWWWWWWWWWWWWWW
WWWWWWWWWWWWWWWWWWWkxXNWWWWWWWNXKKKXWWWWWWWW
WWWWWWWWWWWWWWWWWWWkxXNWWWWWNKx:;,,;lkXWWWWW
WWWWWWWWWWWWWWWWWWMWkxNNWWWNx:;'......,l0WWW
WWWWWWWWWWWWWXKKXNNXdxXNWWWk,.''......'oKWWW
WWWWWWNKxdOOoccllll;:odx0Kl'........,ONWWWN
```

```
NWWWWWWWWWWWWWWWWWWWWWWWWWWWWWWWWWWWWWNNNN
WWWWWWWWWWWWWWWWWWWWWWWWWWWWWWWWWWWWWWWWWNN
WWWWWWWWWWWWWWWWWWWWWWWWWWWWWWWWWWWWWWWWWWW
WWWWWWWWWWWWWWWWWWWWWWWWWWWWWWWWWWWWWWWWWWW
WWWWWWWWWWNXKNWWWWNKOkkk0XKXNWWWWWWWWWWWWWW
WWWWWWWWWWNx:looooo;,,,';c::xNWWWWWWWWWWWWW
WWWWWWWWWWWk;',:ldxo;,,,,;loxKWWWWWWWWWWWWW
WWWWWWWWWWWKl;,lO000xlc:;dXWWWWWWWWWWWWWWWW
WWWWWWWWWWWXx::oO0Ooc::::kWWWWWWWWWWWWWWWWW
WWWWWWWWWWWXxc:lollc;;,;;l0WWWWWWWWWWWWWWWW
WWWWWWWWWWNKKKOl::;;;:ldkXNNNWWWWWWWWWWWWWW
WWWWWWWWWWWWWNWXdc::ldkXNKKNWNNWWWWWWWWWWWW
WWWWWWWWWWWWWWWNOlld0NNWWWWWWWWWWWWWWWWWWWW
WWWWWWWWWWWWWWWWW0xKWWWWWWWWWWWWWWWWWWWWWWW
WWWWWWWWWWWWWWWWWKxKWWWWWWWWWWWWWWWWWWWWWWW
WWWWWWWWWWWWWWWWWKx0WWWWWWWWWWWWWWWWWWWWWWW
WWWWWWWWWWWWWWWWWXx0WWWWWWWWWWWWWWWWWWWWWWW
WWWWWWWWWWWWWWWWWNx0WWWWWWWWWWWWWWWWWWWWWWW
WWWWWWWWWWWWWWWWWNkOWWWWWWWWWWWWWWWWWWWWWWW
WWWWWWWWWWWWWWWWWNkOWMWWWWWWWNNWWWWWWWWWWWW
WWWWWWWWWWWWWWWWWNkOWWWWWWWNOoollokKWWWWWWW
WWWWWWWWWWWWWWWWWNkOWWWWWNkol;,'''';okXWWWWW
WWWWWWWWWNKKKXNNWXxkWWWWWk;,;;,''''.'lKWWWW
WWN0kddxkoc:ccoool:coddOk:',,,,,'..,kNWWWWWW
WKd:,'',,,;:;;;;;;;,,,,:,.',,,',,'.oNWWWWWW
```

```
NNWWWWWWWWWWWWWWWWWWWWWWWWWWWWWWWWWWWNNNNNX
WWWWWWWWWWWWWWWWWWWWWWWWWWWWWWWWWWWWWWWNNNN
WWWWWWWWWWWWWWWWWWWWWWWWWWWWWWWWWWWWWWWWWNN
WWWWWWWWWWWWWWWWWWWWWWWWWWWWWWWWWWWWWWWWWWW
WWWWWWWWWWWWWWWWWWWWWWWWWWWWWWWWWWWWWWWWWWW
WWWWWWWWWWWWWNWWWWWWWWWWWWWWWWWWWWWWWWWWWWW
WWWWWWWWWWWW0dxO0KKKXNWWWWWWWWWWWWWWWWWWWWW
WWWWWWWWWWWWOc;;;::;lkKWWWWWWWWWWWWWWWWWWWW
WWWWWWWWWWWW0c;;;;;,,;oXWWWWWWWWWWWWWWWWWWW
WWWWWWWWWWWWXd::clc;,,;dKWWWWWWWWWWWWWWWWWW
WWWWWWWWWWNKko::okOd:;;:ckNWWWWWWWWWWWWWWWW
WWWWWWWWWWNkc;;:clll::;;,c0WWWWWWWWWWWWWWWW
WWWWWWWWWWWXo::;;::;;:;,;lKNNWWWWWWWWWWWWWW
WWWWWWWWWWWNklc:;;::;::okOOKNNNWWWWWWWWWWWW
WWWWWWWWWWWWNXKOkkdcldkXWNXNWWWWWWWWWWWWWWW
WWWWWWWWWWWWWWWWWW0d0WWWWWWWWWWWWWWWWWWWWWW
WWWWWWWWWWWWWWWWWMKxKMWWWWWWWWWWWWWWWWWWWWW
WWWWWWWWWWWWWWWWWMKxKMWWWWWWWWWWWWWWWWWWWWW
WWWWWWWWWWWWWWWWWMKxKMWWWWWWWWWWWWWWWWWWWWW
WWWWWWWWWWWWWWWWWWKxKMWWWWWWWWWWWWWWWWWWWWW
WWWWWWWWWWWWWWWWWMKxKMWWWWWWWWWWWWWWWWWWWWW
WWWWWWWWWWWWWWWWWMKxKMWWWWWWWWWWWWWWWWWWWWW
WWWWWWWWWWWWWWWWWWKxKMWWWWWWWK000KXWWWWWWWW
WWWWWWWWWWWWWWWWWW0dKMMWWWNXOc;,,,;oONWWWWW
WWWWWWWWWWWWWWWWWW0dKMWWWWO:;;,'....':dKWWW
WWWWNXKXWNXOkkO000dl0XXNWKc'''''.....,dXWWW
WN0dl;;cooc;;;;;;;,,;::lxc'.''.''...cKWWWWW
Ko;,'',,,,;:::::;;,,,,,,'.''''.'''.'kWWWWWW
```

```
WWWWWWWWWWWWWWWWWWWWWWWWWWWWWWWWWWWWWWWWWWWW
WWWWWWWWWWWWWWWWWWWWWWWWWWWWWWWWWWWWWWWWWWWW
WWWWWWWWWWWWWWWWWWWWWWWWWWWWWWWWWWWWWWWWWWWW
WWWWWWWWWWWWWWWWWWWWWWWWWWWWWWWWWWWWWWWWWWWW
WWWWWWWWWWWWWWWWWWWWWWWWWWWWWWWWWWWWWWWWWWWW
WWWWWWWWWWWWWWNNWWWWWWNNNXNWWWWWWWWWWWWWWWWW
WWWWWWWWWWWWKdoxkkkkollccxkx0NWWWWWWWWWWWWWW
WWWWWWWWWWWWKc',;:loc;,,,;;;cONWWWWWWWWWWWWW
WWWWWWWWWWWWXd;;lk00Okd:;cd0KXWWWWWWWWWWWWWW
WWWWWWWWWWWWNkc:ok0Odolc:lKWWWWWWWWWWWWWWWWW
WWWWWWWWWWWNkl:llloc;;,;;xNWWWWWWWWWWWWWWWWW
WWWWWWWWWWWNXK0Kkc::::;:ldKNWWWWWWWWWWWWWWWW
WWWWWWWWWWWWWNNW0o::cco0XK0XNNNWWWWWWWWWWWWW
WWWWWWWWWWWWWWWWXxlok0XWMWWWWWWWWWWWWWWWWWWW
WWWWWWWWWWWWWWWWWXkONWWWWWWWWWWWWWWWWWWWWWWW
WWWWWWWWWWWWWWWWWWOONWWWWWWWWWWWWWWWWWWWWWWW
WWWWWWWWWWWWWWWWWWOOWMWWWWWWWWWWWWWWWWWWWWWW
WWWWWWWWWWWWWWWWWWOOWMWWWWWWWWWWWWWWWWWWWWWW
WWWWWWWWWWWWWWWWWWOOWMWWWWWWWWWWWWWWWWWWWWWW
WWWWWWWWWWWWWWWWWWOOWMWWWWWWWWWWWWWWWWWWWWWW
WWWWWWWWWWWWWWWWWWOOWMWWWWWWWWWWWWWWWWWWWWWW
WWWWWWWWWWWWWWWWWWOOWMWWWWWWWXOkkO0XNWWWWWWW
WWWWWWWWWWWWWWWWMNO0WWWWWWWKkdc:;;;cd0NWWWWW
WWWWWWWWWWNXKXNWWWNk0WWWWW0l:cc;,,;;,;dXWWWW
WWX0OkO0OdlllodxxdldOO0X0o;;;::;,,,,oKWWWWW
NOoc;,;::;:::::::;;;;;:oc',;;,;:;,'lKWWWWWW
```

```
WWWWWWWWWWWWWWWWWWWWWWWWWWWWWWWWWWWWWWWWWWWN
WWWWWWWWWWWWWWWWWWWWWWWWWWWWWWWWWWWWWWWWWWWW
WWWWWWWWWWWWWWWWWWWWWWWWWWWWWWWWWWWWWWWWWWWW
WWWWWWWWWWWWWWWWWWWWWWWWWWWWWWWWWWWWWWWWWWWW
WWWWWWWWWWWWWWWWWWWWWWWWWWWWWWWWWWWWWWWWWWWW
WWWWWWWWWWWWWWWWWWWWWWWWWWWWWWWWWWWWWWWWWWWW
WWWWWWWWWWWWWWWWWWWWWWWWWWWWWWWWWWWWWWWWWWWW
WWWWWWWWWWWWWWWWWWWWWWWWWWWWWWWWWWWWWWWWWWWW
WWWWWWWWWWWWNXNWWWWWWMWWWWWWWWWWWWWWWWWWWWWW
WWWWWWWWXOxkxolodOXWWWWWWWWWWWWWWWWWWWWWWWWW
WWWWWWWNx;cd0ko:;:kWWWWWWWWWWWWWWWWWWWWWWWWW
WWWWWWWWKxx00Kkc;:okXWWWWWWWWWWWWWWWWWWWWWWW
WWWWWWWWWWXKOkdlc::ckXNWWWWWWWWWWWWWWWWWWWWW
WWWWWWWWWNXKKOlcccd0XWWWNNWWWWWWWWWWWWWWWWWW
WWWWWWWWWNNKOKOdxOXWWWWWWWWWWWWWWWWWWWWWWWWW
WWWWWWWWWNWNXNKkONWWWWWWWWWWWWWWWWWWWWWWWWWW
WWWWWWWWWMWWWWNO0WWWWWWWWWWWWWWWWWWWWWWWWWWW
WWWWWWWWWWWWWWW0kNWWWWWWWWWWWWWWWWWWWWWWWWWW
WWWWWWWWWWWWWWMXkKWWWWWWWWWWWWWWWWWWWWWWWWWW
WWWWWWWWWWWWWWWWOONWWWWWWWWWWWWWWWWWWWWWWWWW
WWWWWWWWWWWWWWWWKkXMWWWWWWWWWWWWWWWWWWWWWWWW
WWWWWWWWWWWWWWWMNk0WWWWWWWWWWWWWWWWWWWWWWWWW
WWWWWWWWWWWWWWWWWOONWWWWWWWWWNNNNWWWWWWWWWWW
WWWWWWWWWWWWWWWWWKkXWWWWWWKxolclokKNWWWWWWWW
WWWWWWWWWWWWWWWWWXk0WWWWWXko:;;;,,,;l0WWWWWW
WWWWWWWWWWWNKKXNWNkONWWWNx::::;,,,,'lXWWWWWW
WWWWNK0KXXOdlclodolldxxxc,,',;;;,':0WWWWWWW
WWWKdc;:ooc:::::;;::;,,,,,,,''';:c:,oNWWWWWWW
```

```
WWWWWWWWWWWWWWWWWWWWWWWWWWWWWWWWWWWWWWWWWWW
WWWWWWWWWWWWWWWWWWWWWWWWWWWWWWWWWWWWWWWWWWW
WWWWWWWWWWWWWWWWWWWWWWWWWWWWWWWWWWWWWWWWWWW
WWWWWWWWWWWWWWWWWWWWWWWWWWWWWWWWWWWWWWWWWWW
WWWWWWWWWWWWWNXKKXNWWWWWWWWWWWWWWWWWWWWWWWW
WWWWWWWWWWWWXK00000XWWWWWWWWWWWWWWWWWWWWWWW
WWWWWWWWWWWWXKKKKK0KNWWWWWWWWWWWWWWWWWWWWWW
WWWWWWWWWWWNKKKXXK00XXNWWWWWWWWWWWWWWWWWWWW
WWWWWWWWWWWNXXK0000XNNNXXNNNNWWWWWWWWWWWWWW
WWWWWWWWWWNNNNN0xOKNWWWNXNWNNNWWWWWWWWWWWWW
WWWWWWWWWWNNWWW0xkKNWWWWWWMWWWWWWWWWWWWWWWW
WWWWWWWWWWWWWWWXxxKWWMWWWWWWWWWWWWWWWWWWWWW
WWWWWWWWWWWWWWWNOxKWWWWWWWWWWWWWWWWWWWWWWWW
WWWWWWWWWWWWWWWWXxOWWWWWWWWWWWWWWWWWWWWWWWW
WWWWWWWWWWWWWWWWWkxNWWWWWWWWWWWWWWWWWWWWWWW
WWWWWWWWWWWWWWWWW0xKWWWWWWWWWWWWWWWWWWWWWWW
WWWWWWWWWWWWWWWWWXxOWWWWWWWWWWWWWWWWWWWWWWW
WWWWWWWWWWWWWWWWWNxkWWWWWWWWWWWWWWWWWWWWWWW
WWWWWWWWWWWWWWWWWWOxXMWWWWWWWWWWWWWWWWWWWWW
WWWWWWWWWWWWWWWWWW0dKMWWWWMWKkxxxxOXWWWWWWW
WWWWWWWWWWWWWWWWWWXdOMWWWWX0o;,'..';lk0NWWW
WWWWWWWWWWWWWWWWWWNxkWWWWXo;;;,'..'...lXWWW
WWWWWWNNWWNXOkkO0K0ookOKXx;'',,'....,dXWWWW
WWWXOollodo:;;;;;:;,,,,,;;'....'''..oNWWWWW
WWXd;,',,,,,,;;;;,,'''''''''...'',,''xWWWWWW
```

Evil Key's computers and servers were corrupted and useless. But the moment they actually won was when Centimuss activated the explosives causing the solar batteries to explode, causing solar explosions and supernovas which then caused the black hole generator to explode, making a gigantic black hole that consumed Evil Key's entire base. At that moment, they tasted the sweet flavor of victory that warriors eternally yearn for.

LIII. The Battle Won

"This calls for a celebration, in the honor of Rust and his sacrifice," Infinity said.

"Seriously! Now? The man just died and you want to celebrate?!?" Nat exclaimed in disbelief.

"Well, that man was a version of me. And I don't like anybody to be gloomy on the day I die, especially if I died to save someone or to cause a victory!" Infinity replied sheepishly.

"Okay then, in the honor of Rust" replied Nat.

"In the honor of Rust," said both Joy and Centimuss.

"I'm going to whip up some Champagne, you all coming?" Joy said.

They all headed into the living room started preparing party necessities.

Centimuss dimmed the lights making it into 'party mood'. Nat took out some soft drinks and some food and snacks, such as chips, mini sandwiches and a couple boxes of pizza. Infinity went and put on some soothing music.

They all gathered around the couch. Nat and Joy put the food and drinks and plates on the table and they toasted Rust and held a moment of silence for him. They all started talking to each other.

Whilst Centimuss and Joy were catching up Infinity chatted with Nat. They were enjoying their food and drinks whilst talking, taking chips here and there and the occasional sip from their drinks.

"So what now? Are you going to go back home or do you want to continue your dimension hopper life?" Infinity asked.

"Sadly, I have to go. These past days were very tiring even though I have had a great time and learnt immensely. I do not know how to thank you!" Nat replied.

"There is no need, it was a pleasure having you. And there isn't much more you can do that can excite you like this," Infinity replied.

Infinity and Nat continued talking about their glory times during the adventures they had had. Infinity stopped the music and started singing * memories - David Guetta ft. Kid Cudi *. The rest started singing along with him. They were all enjoying the moment. After the song, they swapped who they were talking to, and Centimuss started talking with Nat and Joy with Infinity.

"I was wondering do you want to move in with me? I have plenty of rooms. I felt terrible you were all alone!" Infinity asked Joy.

"Only if you want me to. I don't wish to intrude on your privacy," Joy replied.

"I would most certainly be honored, my lady!" Infinity replied

They both chuckled and continued talking for a while, catching up and listening to each other's adventures.

Later on, they again mixed up with whom they were talking to. Joy started talking with Nat while Infinity and Centimuss went aside and started talking to each other.

"You're not acting like yourself. You looked worried. Start acting like you are at a party, even though for some there is no difference," Centimuss perceptively said.

Infinity laughed and said "Remember one year ago I told you to make backups of yourself and spread them out,"

"I do and did so but the story is far from over, isn't it?" Centimuss said.

Infinity nodded.

"Well how is he going to come here, he can't just vibrate to here. We have systems to prevent people from doing that!" Centimuss said.

"Rust forgot to give his keys," Infinity replied.

"Well how soon is he going to be a problem again?" Centimus asked.

Suddenly the alarms were set off and the lights went out and the emergency lights turned on.

"That soon," said Infinity.

LIV. The battle lost

A huge explosion was heard.

Centimuss checked the status of the base and said: “Left main hall is down, I am shutting it off.”

Centimuss managed to shut off the left main hall.

All of the monitors suddenly went black and then showed Evil Key’s mask with an old VHS effect, making random faces, the crack on it still there. He started singing * berserk – Eminem* causing all the monitors and security system to malfunction except for the main lock which had an entirely separate system. There were sparks flying everywhere from the malfunctioning devices.

Evil Key started coming out from the main tunnel.

“Nice place!! I could get used to this after this is all over. ! As you may have heard, since it was awfully loud, my base somehow got completely destroyed,” Evil Key said.

Infinity told Nat and Joy to go to safety and asked Joy to take care of Nat.

Joy and Nat rushed towards their rooms, unlocking the door and closing it firmly behind themselves.

“I will be coming for you later!” Evil Key said. His attention reverted back to Infinity.

“Oh, I have a bone to pick with you first,” Evil Key said.

He calmly walked towards Infinity and Centimuss. Centimuss attempted to punch him but he just broke his own arm and Evil Key kicked his body to the side. Then he shot Centimuss, destroying that body.

“No don’t” Infinity said as Centimuss tried to deflect the punch But it was too late.

Evil Key started singing * look what you made me do - Taylor Swift * and went on and fought Infinity, having the upper hand. The body that he had now was stronger and faster than the last one. Infinity could not focus enough to sing a song so it could help him. He was too tired from the last time he fought him.

As the song finished, Evil Key had defeated him and Infinity fell aside. Evil Key did not kill him though.

"Once you took away from me, what was precious to me. Because I'm such a splendid guy, I'll give you this deal. You bring your original body to the place that it all started, where we started and I promise that I will let your precious friends leave and I will not go after your precious Nat. Who do you love more? Yourself or others? You have one day. Adios amigo!"

Evil Key hit Infinity in the head knocking him out.

LV. Madness

Nat and Joy were behind the closed door, within the vaults, thinking that they were safe enough, when they heard the song *animal - Maroon 5*. The song was coming from Evil Key. The song had given him sharp claws and had enhanced his speed, strength and agility. He broke through the vaults like as if it was made of aluminum foil.

He started chasing them, going from room to room. At times, due to his high speed, he would run on the walls, toying with Joy and Nat, as if they were mice. Centimuss was trying to stop the music with the base's defense system but Evil Key was evading them as if they were non-existent.

Eventually, they reached Infinity's memory server room. To Centimuss' horror Evil Key began to destroy the beloved servers there. In the server room Evil Key managed to corner Joy. Joy tried to put up a fight but was easily knocked out by Evil Key.

Evil Key then continued hunting down Nat, through the hallway of the rooms. At the beginning of the hallway he started singing * madness – Ruelle *. The song caused Nat to start hallucinating. She began to see every single thing that she feared marching towards her, slowly flowing out of the rooms. Evil Key calmly started walking towards her, as she was dragging herself back in fear. She accidentally dropped her satchel in the hallway and she ran into her room. Evil Key seemingly paid no attention to the satchel and passed it,, slowly getting closer and closer to her room.

She locked her room and tried to open up a portal but couldn't. Evil Key came behind her. The song finished.

Nat ran to a corner, Evil Key slowly walking towards her, reaching out for her necklace. The necklace made a forcefield around her, andEvil

Key pushed harder to reach it, as his clothes kept getting repelled back. He kept forcing himself closer to her, to the point that his skin and flesh was peeling off his hands. Nat felt vulnerable and helpless. Trapped! Evil Key finally caught ahold ofthe necklace and yanked it off her neck, throwing the neckless aside. His clothes went back on to his arm and hand, covering the bloody mess which had been caused.

He hit her, knocking her out, and picked up her body and began to leave the base. Whilst he was walking down the hallway, he threw an EMP grenade causing the whole power system of the base to shut down. The EMP caused Centimuss' power to shut down resulting in him to also shut down. Only silence and darkness remained. And Infinity.

LVI. Prospective

Nat woke up, finding herself in the most unagreeable position of being tied up to a pole, sitting on the floor. She had a terrible headache. She was in a rather large makeshift shed. There was a device on her wrist, which stopped her from using any of her tech and give her an extreme feeling of fatigue. She also did not have her satchel of wonders. Evil Key was sitting in front of her on a chair, staring at her.

"Finally, it only took 9 hours for you to wake up!" Evil Key said.

"Why are you keeping me alive?" Nat asked.

"Shocker, I know! It's because I'm a man of my word" Evil Key responded.

"Why are you doing this? Don't you feel anything?" Nat asked.

Evil Key's mask made a face as if it was thinking and he replied "Hmmm might be because …. ,"

Evil Key started singing *Bad-Royale Deluxe*, whilst doing a dance and creating a light and image show behind him, in synch with his song.

After Evil Key song was finished, Nat said: "No I don't think you're saying the complete truth! There's something that is haunting you, isn't there?"

"Of course, there has been a lot of truths that hasn't been said. But I'm the monster which wants to listen to me," Evil Key replied in aggressive tone.

"It is not that cut and dry. You don't have to do this. Let me loose and we can talk about this. I will listen to your side!" Nat replied.

"My side?", he laughed and said louder: "My bloody side! It is none of your God damn business! There has only been one man who ever understood me and he didn't even fully understand me!" Evil Key exclaimed.

"Why do you wear a mask?" Nat asked.

"Why do you wear clothes?" Evil Key responded.

"Why do you call yourself Evil Key?" Nat replied.

"Were you not listening to me? Because I want to! And what is it with you, asking so many questions?" Evil Key snarled.

Evil Key looked look down and laughed. He looked back at Nat and said: "You know, you're just like me!! You like to get inside people's heads; to see what makes them tick. You study them. You are just like me. Well, at least you have the potential! "

Nat just stared at him and then quietly replied, in an aggrieved tone:"I'm nothing like you. I don't like to kill, like you. I don't enjoy seeing others pain, like you. I'm nothing like you!"

"No! No! No! I can see it in you. You just have to give into your shadow. Anybody can give into their shadow but some are destined to be great at it, to become legends! Just like you and me!" Evil Key gleefully replied.

Evil Key started singing *natural - imagine dragons*. He was interrupted by Nat in midcourse.

He stopped singing and shouted at Nat: "SHUT UP OR I WILL SEW YOUR MOUTH SHUT "

He continued singing the song and finished it.

"Don't you have any manners? Go ahead, yap away!" Evil Key said.

"Infinity and the rest are going to come and save me!" Nat said.

Evil Key pulled his chair closer to Nat and said "Oh, I'm counting on him to come. If he doesn't, well, let's just say that I will have to dispose of you."

Evil Key looked at his wrist as if there was a watch there and continued saying "You have about ten hours left. Either Hero Key will show up and I can finally get rid of him or he will not show up, meaning I have finally broken him. It's a win-win situation for me. By the way, his name is Hero Key!! Infinity, what a stupid name,"

"Anyway, you must be hungry!" Evil Key said after a few moments

"Yes I am, actually," Nat replied,

"Well that's a shame. Ciao!" Evil Key replied.

Evil Key stood up and left. Leaving Nat alone, hungry, in a makeshift shed.

LVII. Value

Infinity was woken up by the sound of Joy singing * need me – Eminem ft. P!nk *. Infinity started singing the song with her. The song was energizing him.

After the song finished, Joy quietly said "Evil Key took her." She then gave him Nat's satchel.

Thirteen hours had passed since the attack. Infinity quickly rushed into the gadgets room, picking up some solar batteries. Infinity went to Centimuss' room and put batteries in the sockets powering Centimuss. Centimuss made himself a new body.

They all went into the living room, Infinity and Joy taking out icepack and nursing their bruises with them.

Centimuss was reviewing the status of the base and said "Well that was some party!! The power room was shut down. The left main hall is badly damaged. Your server room has been destroyed and there's a lot of damage to the security system. Most monitors are destroyed, the vaults are destroyed, most devices are destroyed, and your clones have been exterminated. There are scratches and claw marks all over the place, but the good news is that my servers and computers have not been touched."

Infinity was silent, thinking by himself.

"What is it? You haven't said a word," Joy asked.

"He said, he will leave you all alone and lets Nat go if I give him my original body," Infinity said.

"As tempting as that may sound to you, you have to say no," Centimuss said.

"You obviously have to say, no! We will find another way to save Nat," Joy said.

"I can't, he said he will kill her in 11 hours. I have no choice," Infinity said.

Infinity started singing *we are the Champions – queen* trying to reassure them. It helped a bit but not that much. It rang rather hollow.

The sorrow in both Joy's and Centimuss eyes was obvious.

"I recognize, it is your choice. We cannot make you decide anything but...," Centimuss said

"Then you already know what I'm going to choose," Infinity replied.

Both Centimuss and Joy hugged Infinity. Infinity hugged them back very emotionally. He knew he would miss them and that they will miss him. Joy started singing *truce – twenty one pilots*.

"I better get my body. Centimuss, can you be a dear?" Infinity said.

From the speakers, a very glitched out voice blasted: 1-hour encoding activated in 3, 3, 3, 3... 2... 1... 1... 1...

T@###%*&u^%(^c$%^h^%((eh%^$*&$*e$$$$did#@@#!ki$%^#ll$%^h
^$##i**^&m&^&%&se&^%^&lf&^%$#%$#@i!!#!nt^$^$^h^$e*^&^pr*
^$$#oc*%$%&esss+==)ol!%^$te^&$%^$chn&$^$^$^$@@ic^^)^^%ally!
%!%%!stil*&^%$lha@%#@vea$##$%#@cha3523521@%@%nc#%#%@
ew5#@%@hat#$%#@th#^%#%ehe#^#$%llis#^%#$%hes$#^%$ayin$^$
g

LVIII. Mirror

Fkcfkfqv txp qefkhfkd ql efjpbic "dlpe, qefp cbbip pqrmfa, yrq fq'p clo qebj, xka clo ebo."

fkcfkfqv txihba qeolrde qeb exiitxvp ql efp olljp xka pqxoqba qefkhfkd xylrq xii lc qeb dobxq qfjbp eb exa exa xka efp obdobqp; qeb qefkdp eb pqfii txkqba ql al yrq tlria klq dbq xolrka ql al, xp eb

eb afa klq cbbi pxa lo xkdov. Kl cbxo. Eb cbiq jlpqiv xq bxpb xka zxij, xp fc eb exa zljb ql qbojp tfqe qefp jljbkq jxkv vbxop xdl. Eb txp obxav ql afb. Eb afa klq cbxo abxqe. Mboexmp eb bsbk tbizljba fq.

kbsboqebibpp, xp eb bkqboba efp ollj, eb cbiq x yfq xkuflrp, dbqqfkd kbxobo xka kbxobo ql efp lofdfkxi ylav yrq eb lsbozxjb fq. Eb cfopq mfzhba rm x mfbzb lc mxmbo xka mbk xka tolqb pljbqefkd mrqqfkd fq fkql qeb pxqzebi. Kbuq, eb tbkq fk colkq lc qeb jfoolo fk efp ollj xka pqxoqba pfkdfkd *man in the mirror - Michael Jackson*, tfqe dobxq bjlqflkxi. Lkzb qeb plkd bkaba, x pbzobq ollj lmbkba.

piltiv eb txihba fkpfab fq xka fq zilpba ybefka efj.

qebob txp klq qexq jrze ollj fkpfab qeb efaabk ollj yrq fq txp ilkd. Fq exa x kxoolt xfpib, cfiiba tfqe qebpb qolmev pqxkap. Tebk vlr txihba fkpfab qeb ollj fq tlria peofkh vlr fk pfwb jxhfkd fq pbbj yfddbo. Fq txp cfiiba tfqe fkcfkfqv'p qobxprobp; qeb qefkdp qexq eb xppfdkba jlob sxirb ql qexk qeb obpq. Objkxkqp lc qfjbp mxpq qexq eb exa ifsba. Qebob txp x pfkdib sxq fk qeb zbkqbo lc qeb zljmxoqjbkq tfqe x ylav cilxqfkd fkpfab lc fq -- fkcfkfqv'p lofdfkxi ylav qexq exa ybbk mobpbosba clo xii qebpb vbxop.

fkcfkfqv mrq efp exka xdxfkpq qeb txii obsbxifkd x pbzobq zljmxoqjbkq zlkqxfkfkd x exoa afph zlkqxfkfkd jbjlofbp -- qeb jbjlofbp qexq fkcfkfqv txkqba ql exsb tefib eb txp avfkd.

mxppfkd yv efp jlpq mofwba lygbzqp, eb objbjyboba qeb qfjbp eb dlq qebj lo bxokba qebj xka qeb pqlofbp qebv exa ybefka qebj: x dobbk txqze qexq eb exa jxab, x melkb, x ptloa qexq eb exa lkzb abpfdkba; fqbjp colj efp mobsflrp obixqflkpefmp; melqlp lc efp ilsba lkbp, ifhb glv xka efp ilsb, efp cxjfiv, efp cofbkap; xipl melqlp colj efp xasbkqrobp tefze tebk eb mxppba yv qebj txp xp fc eb txp qebob; fqbjp colj qeb qfjbp qexq eb exa ilpq. Pljb, eb zlria kl ilkdbo objbjybo. Pljb lc qeb pqrcc qexq eb exa mxppba tebob,

fkcfkfqv obxzeba qeb sxq. Ybefka qeb sxq txp x absfzb telpb mromlpb txp ql qoxkpmloq qeb zljmibqb ollj fc qeb yxpb txp ybfkd abpqolvba ql x pxcb ilzxqflk. Lk qeb ibcq qebob txp x qltbi exkdbo tfqe x cliaba qltbi qebob. Lk qeb ofdeq qebob txp x zljmrqbo xka kbuq ql fq qeb ifcb-prmmloq. Fkcfkfqv fkpboqba x rpy cixpe fkql qeb zljmrqbo xka pqxoqba fjmloqfkd qelpb jbjlofbp ql qeb lofdfkxi ylav'p yoxfk. Fkcfkfqv qllh qefp absfzb xka mrq fq lk efp ebxa zlmvfkd qeb jbjlofbp qexq eb exa xka dfsfkd qebj ql qeb lofdfkxi ylav.

fkcfkfqv cbii ql qeb cillo bjlqflkxiiv eb pqxoqba illhfkd rm xq qeb sxq.

efp ofkd ybdxk x zlrkqaltk: ljbdx fk 3... 2... 1...

ah ah ah ah ah ah ah ah ah ah ah reve naht redab dna regnorts kcab eb lliw I ho ah ah ah ah ssenkrad erom eb syaw lla lliw ereht tub thgil eb ereht teL

LIX. Courage

Infinity was on the floor, lying on the floor in front of the vat containing the original body.

The original body was completely nude. Besides that, there was a severed robotic hand, as the body was missing its left hand. It had very long though receding, dark brown hair, bordering on dark blue., The body was around 6.1feet tall, with skin color that was white but slightly tanned. It had straight white teeth, dark brown eyes and the body was generally lean and muscular. The body was still unconscious.

Infinity was looking up at the body.

"Well Buddy, we have finally reached the end of the rope. I'm sorry I have given you such a miserable time!" he said to his original body.

Infinity then started singing * bitter end – Rag'n'Bone * rather emotionally.

This choice was not easy for Infinity but he knew he had made the right choice.

The body regained its consciousness. With all the memories that Infinity had also copied into him, he was slightly confused since he had just woken up, after such a long time. He started banging on the vat. Infinity pressed a button, causing the vat to release all of its fluids and afterwards it opened up.

The original body came out. He looked at Infinity then started looking around. He noticed the towel rack and took the towel and dried himself off. "Mind if I have my clothes back," he croaked.

"I'm so sorry, I didn't mean any of this to happen," Infinity said.

The original body looked at him and said: “I have your memories; you are me and I am you. To whom are lying? We both know that it was not our fault but still we want to punish ourselves for it!”

Infinity stood up and touched him on the shoulder. He started singing * dress - Taylor Swift * transferring his clothes onto him. Infinity gave him the ring as well. With the original body fully clothed Infinity was completely naked. The original body chose the default version of the clothes, with the golden key logo on his chest.

“Welcome back Hero Key,” The ring said.

“Do it painlessly, please,” Infinity said.

The original body nodded. He started singing * mirrors - Justin Timberlake * transferring the last thoughts, emotions, memories of Infinity to himself. The original body was now the only Infinity. All of the other clone bodies had been destroyed the servers were destroyed. This was Infinity/Hero Key’s last life.

Infinity went out of the secret room back to the living room were Joy and Centimuss were waiting for him.

He entered the room. Both of them turned around looking at him.

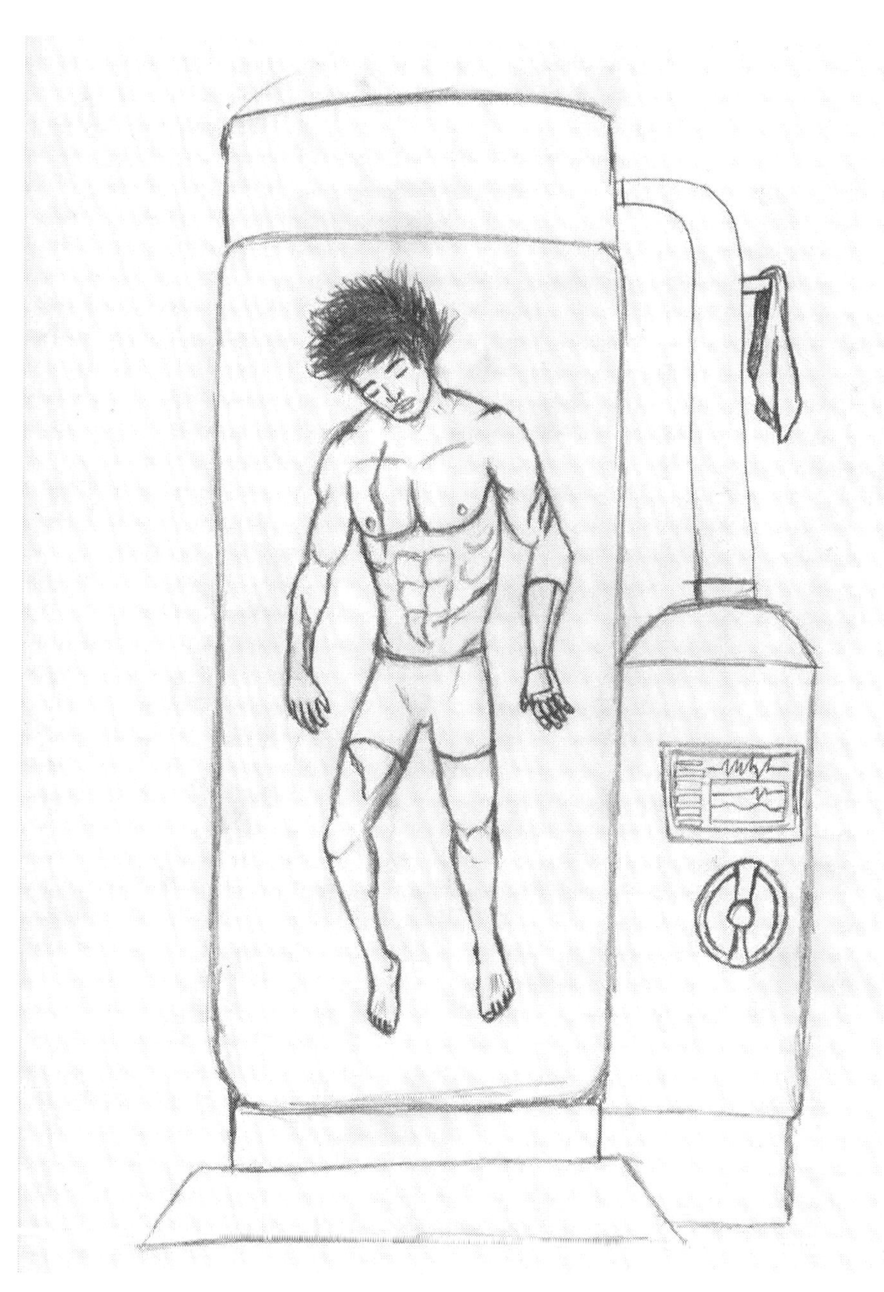

LX. To Lose It All

Infinity started singing * Rain – Rag'n'Bone *, Joy joined in as well. The song finished.

Infinity hugged her and went and hugged Centimuss next.

"You know how I am with emotions. I just can't process them," Centimuss said.

Centimuss quickly rushed and hugged Infinity, crying, as he hugged him.

"Just lost one of the people I adored. I can't believe, I am losing another one," Centimuss said.

"Thank you for being with me for all these years. I'm sorry for all the troubles I caused you. I'm sorry for all the pain I brought with myself. I am though eternally grateful I had such wonderful people like you two in my life. I'm sorry for what I'm going to do and for breaking your hearts," Infinity said to the two of them.

"No don't be sorry! Thank you for giving life to me. Thank you for listening to me. Thank you for believing in me. Thank you for noticing, we had our own emotions. Thank you for considering me a conscience being and giving me my body," Joy cried.

"Thank you for making the British. Thank you for making me brilliant and witty. Thank you for making me the smartest being in the Multi-verse. Thank you for giving me complex emotions, those were very helpful indeed" Centimuss said hysterically.

Centimuss looked down and said in a serious tone: "Thank you for building me. Thank you for listening to me. Thank you for considering me a person. Thank you for giving me a choice. Thank you for letting me stay. Thank you for making me feel special."

Infinity hugged them both once more in a group hug. All three of them were very emotional.

Centimuss wiping d away a tear said "So this is your goodbye? You always like to make it very emotional, don't you? Just like series finales!"

Infinity responded with singing * no good and goodbye - the scripts *.

"I'm sure going to miss your singing. No matter how cheesy or great the songs you chose were!" Joy replied.

"When I'm gone. Please take care of Nat. Also please teach her how to use her ring. And give her satchel back to her," Infinity asked.

Infinity gave the satchel to them. Both Centimuss and Joy nodded their heads.

Infinity sighed and said "So here's the plan. It's going to take place where the genocide happened. I want to try to sneak in and release Nat. I will most probably get caught and get attacked. We will then talk afterwards and will probably have another fight. That is when I need you two to come in and save Nat and leave. I will most probably lose the fight and die because this body is weak but I'm going to try to kill him with me. What you too must do is come with me but in spectator mode. Once the fight starts, you take Nat and leave!!"

Infinity gave a piece of paper containing Rusts base location with its password to Centimuss. Centimuss scanned it and then gave it to Joy. Joy sorted it onto her ring.

"Go to Rust's base if you want to try to rebuild here. I recommend laying low for a while. Also Rust's dog, Star, is at his base. Go get her as well. We only have a few hours left and we should get going," Infinity continued saying.

While they were going to the transport room Joy sang *victory – Pagadixx ft. Malee" whilst prepping them all up and it make Infinity feel better and more energized.

They got to the room. Joy put herself and Centimuss into spectator mode. Infinity shrunk them all down and opened up a small portal and they all left. The small portal closed behind them one last time.

LXI. Nothing to Lose

A small portal opened inside the middle of the crater. Infinity enlarged Joy and Centimuss, back to their normal size, who promptly went and hid. Infinity saw the shed in the distance and walked cautiously up the crater towards it. He entered it and instantly saw Nat, sitting there on the ground, starving, thirsty and tired.

Infinity climbed up delicately to her ear and whispered: "I am here to break you out, don't draw any attention to me."

Nat noticed and heard Infinity and gave no reaction. She continued her same behavior, the little that it was, given her circumstances.

Infinity first broke the device preventing her from using her items. Next, whilst untying Nat from the post, he accidentally set off an alarm inside the cuffs. Evil Key jumped up and kicked open the doors of the shed.

"You used to say hello. It is a shame that you never learned your manners. I guess you don't believe in the saying 'better late than never'!" Evil Key yelled out.

Infinity enlarged himself back to his normal size. He was standing behind Nat.

"Hello Hero. And they say I'm the one with no manners! Going back to your own style I see," Evil Key said.

"You promised you would let her go if I came in my original body," Infinity said.

"Exactly. I promised I would, let her go, not let you try to free her. For that I might just shoot her," Evil Key replied.

Evil Key pointed his ring at Nat preparing to shoot. Infinity instantly activated a freeze spell on Evil Key, freezing him in place in a block of ice. He was about to activate another spell but was interrupted in the middle of it by Evil Key, who managed to break the spell.

Evil Key started singing *dark horse - Katy Perry ft. juicy J*. Infinity was now frozen in place. Evil Key started walking towards him to do the things that he sang about. When the first chorus began he grabbed Infinity's face. A red-eyed dark horse was constructed. . It started stamping towards Infinity, hitting him and bursting through the other side of the shed's wall. Then a red-eyed dark hawk wi was constructed and stroke Infinity from the sky. At the end of song, Evil Key sent the horse one more time towards Infinity. If Infinity did not have the clothes he was wearing, he would have been dead by now.

Nat ran check on Infinity, then noticed his face.

"Dad?!?!" gasped Nat.

LXII. Behind the Masks

"Dad? When did you become a father? What does this mean? Is she the one who's going to die and you will runway? Or you're going to die and then how is she going to be born? This is quite a conundrum!" Evil Key asked, visibly confused.

Infinity stood up and replied "No running away. This is just between you and me."

"When did you get all so brave and tough again? I'd like to return you back to the time when you were in your scared and pathetic stage!" Evil Key said.

"Look who's talking, the person who is so afraid that hides behind a cracked mask that he could easily repair. Who hides behind lies that he tells himself. Who hates himself so much, that he doesn't want to see his own face!" Infinity replied.

"You're right, your daughter deserves to know who I am!" Evil Key said.

Evil Key puts his hand on his mask. His helmet started deforming until it was only the mask. He then pulls the mask away with a flourish, his face being one and the same as Infinity's original body.

"See child, I am a version of your dad, who was never good enough for him. What a wretched rascal I am. Which destiny had set me out to be the villain? Even so I accepted it. I embraced it. All because of some inane and arbitrary factors that differed in your father and I. He accepted others' company, whilst I pushed them away. He didn't want to kill, but I saw it as the better choice. He was loved, but no one loves me. So the Multiverse, at least this one, decided I should be a monster while he should be the hero," Evil Key said in his normal voice.

Evil Key put his mask back on and the helmet started to reform around his head. This time repairing the crack on the face but keeping the glitches on the face. His voice went back to the it's robotic glitchy version.

Evil Key opened a portal to a paradoxical dimension. Not just any old paradoxical dimension but to the one that was the opposite of their original dimension.

"I am a man of my word, unlike you. If you go through this portal, I'll leave your friends alone and let Nat go," Evil Key said.

Infinity starts walking towards the portal and then suddenly halted and said: "Yes, you *are* a man of your word but you never said that she can leave alive."

Evil Key began a slow clap and laughed: "You know me too well, don't you? As they say, 'Great minds think alike'!"

Infinity quickly shot at Evil Key causing an enormous blast that blew him away. The blast at first was spiral with multiple colors, each wave hitting Evil Key separately. Then they all converged into one great wave, which threw him even further away. At the same time the surge of excess energy was empowering Infinity, making him instantly stronger and faster, energizing him. It was made him glow very brightly.

"I had been charging that ever since I met Nat!" Infinity replied.

LXIII. Hope

Evil Key stood up. Most of his clothes had burned off. His skin was completely burnt. His mask was again cracked, this time so badly that his eye could be seen through the crack, and the helmet and mask began to fragment causing them to fall off his face and shatter on the ground. A very angry face could be seen on him. Evil Key's voice went back to his normal voice.

"Every single time! Every single bloody time? You never allow me to fully enjoy my victory," Evil Key shouted.

Evil Key flew towards Infinity as he gained acceleration. Infinity too started flying towards him. Infinity began singing * bleeding out - imagine dragons * which caused him to gain even more acceleration. When they came close to each other, they punched each other in their respective faces. Evil Key was continuously thrown back, getting punched back by Infinity who was in a blaze of emotions.

Centimuss and Joy after seeing the fight begin knew it was their que. They had quickly opened a portal to the left of the shed and were now struggling to get Nat to leave with them. "We can't just leave him," she cried as they pushed her through the portal. The portal closed and Nat burst into tears.

The song finished. Both Evil Key and Infinity landed. Evil Key tumbled down to the ground while Infinity landed hard but sturdlly. Evil Key was badly bruised and bloodied, with a black eye, despite having a body more durable than his previous bodies and far more durable than Infinity's original body.

Evil Key stood up and said: "Do you really think them running away will save them? I will just hunt them down again and again!"

"I know you will, so that's why this has to end here!" Infinity replied.

“Stop acting like a coward and fights me hand-to-hand!” Evil Key taunted.

Infinity had only enough energy to keep himself energized and to keep his stamina up.

Infinity started singing * my way - Frank Sinatra * and the song caused him to become strong enough and fast enough so he could actually compete with Evil Key. They started wrestling and boxing each other to the ground.

They were both getting hit and successfully landing damaging hits on each other. Sometimes Infinity managed to dodge Evil Key’s blows whilst Evil Key sometimes blocked Infinity’s blows.

The song finished and they were both breathless. They were tired, badly damaged, bruised and bloody. It was a fight to the death and they were most equally matched.

“After I kill you, your friends are next, then our own dimension,” Evil Key said.

“I believe you,” Infinity replied.

“Don’t you dare think of doing that,” Evil Key said.

Infinity looked up and smiled. Infinity flew towards Evil Key with great speed holding him and not letting him go, using up the rest of his energy by preventing him from trying to escape. They were heading to the portal, which led to the paradoxical dimension.

As they pushed and heaved ever closer to the portal, Infinity was at peace with himself while Evil Key was struggling to get out of Infinity’s clutches and shouting “No don’t do this, we will both be destroyed!”, “I’m sorry I won’t hunt them down!”, “It is not going to be a happy ending, you’re better than this,” ,“You know what will happen if you get rid of me completely!!” For a while, he just screamed until they went into the portal. Prior to them entering the portal Infinity’s ring flew off his finger with great speed, faster and faster, from dimension to dimension but Evil Key's ring entered with him.

They entered into the portal and the portal closed behind them for the last time.

LXIV. Infinity

Nat was on her knees still crying. She still hadn't come to terms with Infinity's death. Her father's death. Joy gave Nat her satchel back. Nat thanked Joy and put it round her neck it. Quickly taking something out to drink since she hadn't eaten or drunken for a long time, she noticed a note in one of the slots of the satchel. She first took out a bottle of water and drank it, afterward she took out the note to read.

It was from her father, it said:

"Hello darling, so now you know, who I am by now. I know you must be heartbroken, since you believe I'm dead and all. Don't worry though, your father is still alive. Yes I know I caused a paradox but if we're lucky the Multi-verse will fix it – well half of it at least. You still have to learn how to use your ring. Joy is going to help you with that. I'm afraid that there might be some threats for you still out there.
*Centimuss and Joy are going to take care of you. I want you all to stay low and together for a while, just for your safety. Your dimension should be safe now. I'm glad that I at least managed to save you. Remember that song *do you realize - the flaming lips * if you don't give it a listen. It might help you. Anyways I have to be going now. I don't have that much time. I've been waiting for a long time to say this. I love you my baby girl! Xoxo. Love from∞ "*

She wept silently a bit more but slowly stopped.

Centimuss came to her and said "Come on, we are not safe here."

Nat put away the note lovingly in the satchel and stood up and went with Centimuss and Joy to Rust's base. She stopped crying and instead hummed the melody of "do you realize-The Flaming lips". They opened the portal and entered through it.

Meanwhile, Infinity had just flown towards Evil Key and grabbed him and held him tight. He was thinking to himself His last thoughts:

"Well, this must be the most stupid thing I've ever done. It is all for her though. Keep your eye on the prize. Evil Key is quite worried, I guess he hasn't accepted that it is his time yet. Maybe some songs will make these last minutes more peaceful." Infinity thought of the song *carry on wayward son – Kansas * but stopped thinking about it after the first verse. "No, I don't want the last thing to remember to be the show Supernatural... how dare he say that. I am not going to rip off someone else's series finale, which was about feelings and mine is about... feelings. Okay, I can see some similarities but every story and worlds like that, every story has been told over and over again. It is just different versions of the same one. I guess that's the glory to it. That everything repeats itself. Just like the hero's story and we're drawn to it because it is like our own stories. It could also be our nostalgic thoughts about those stories. I'm getting quite close. I got it I know what song to play," Infinity starts thinking of * knock'in on heaven's door - Bob Dylan *. As the song finished Infinity was only a few seconds away from the portal. "Hey, there goes my ring. Any second now." Infinity and Evil Key entered the portal. "Oh, it doesn't kill me instantly. I guess it takes me apart first from decision to decision. Hey, it's actually getting darker. Before I get to do anything else... ,"

Infinity said his last words:

"Let there be Light…"

Printed in Great Britain
by Amazon